THE PENITENT

DE WOLFE CONNECTED WORLD

CATHY MACRAE

De Wolfe Pack: The Series

By Aileen Fish
The Duke She Left Behind

By Alexa Aston
Rise of de Wolfe

By Amanda Mariel
Love's Legacy
One Wanton Wager

By Anna Markland
Hungry Like de Wolfe

By Ashe Barker
Wolfeheart

By Autumn Sands
Reflection of Love

By Barbara Devlin
Lone Wolfe: Heirs of Titus De Wolfe Book 1
The Big Bad De Wolfe: Heirs of Titus De Wolfe Book 2
Tall, Dark & De Wolfe: Heirs of Titus De Wolfe Book 3

By Cathy MacRae
The Saint
The Penitent

By Christy English
Dragon Fire

By Danelle Harmon
Heart of the Sea Wolfe

By Hildie McQueen
The Duke's Fiery Bride

By Kathryn Le Veque
River's End

By Lana Williams
Trusting the Wolfe

By Laura Landon
A Voice on the Wind

By Leigh Lee
Of Dreams and Desire

By Mairi Norris
Brabanter's Rose

By Marlee Meyers
The Fall of the Black Wolf

By Mary Lancaster
Vienna Wolfe
The Wicked Wolfe

By Meara Platt

Nobody's Angel

Kiss an Angel

Bhrodi's Angel

By Mia Pride

The Lone Wolf's Lass

By Michele Lang

An Honest Woman

By Ruth Kaufman

My Enemy, My Love

My Rebel, My Love

By Sarah Hegger

Bad Wolfe on the Rise

By Scarlett Cole

Together Again

By Victoria Vane

Breton Wolfe Book 1

Ivar the Red Book 2

The Bastard of Brittany Book 3

By Violetta Rand

Never Cry de Wolfe

THE PENITENT

Simon de Bretteby is one of The Saint's closest friends and most loyal soldiers. His entire life has revolved around service to Lord de Wolfe's nephew—except for one summer when he was ordered across the Scottish border to put a stop to a rogue chieftain who'd stolen cattle from an English lord. Injured and separated from his men, de Bretteby had little chance of survival, but a kind-hearted Scottish lass boldly healed his body, though he left his heart in her keeping.

Iseabal Maxwell, daughter of Chief Maxwell's bastard son, has little love for English soldiers—and even less love for clan politics. With her sister ordered to wed as a pawn for peace along the Border, Iseabal expects the same bleak future. As relations between the two nations grows ever more strained, defying her father's orders by saving the life of an English knight risked much. But letting him go was the hardest thing she has ever done.

Now her life lies in ruins—her father dead after the English besieged their home, her fate decided by a man she fears. What will happen when she appears on Simon's doorstep, carrying secrets she would die to protect?

www.cathymacraeauthor.com

Words of Interest

Bausie (Ewan's pony) = a well-fleshed animal

Billies = male companions, lively young fellows

Daupit = stupid, imbecile

Drue (Iseabal's horse) = Greek for courageous, strong

Feardie = a coward

Fuddelt = drunk

Frowe = a big, buxom woman

Hogget = a sheep 1-3 years of age

Ill-gotten wean = illegitimate child

Nacket = a precious child

Oxter = arm pit

Radgie = rowdy, randy

Wee chield = a small child, usually a boy

Wick = a naughty child

Wratch = a wretch

PROLOGUE

Along the River Annan near Lockardebi, Scotland
North of the Border
March, 1235

H EW'S LEGS TREMBLED as he slid from the back of the cart. The driver gave a grunt and a nod at the elder's mumbled thanks before clucking to his team and driving away. The gate to the Maxwell's keep was shut tight, the tower house beyond rising darkly from the silent yard.

What in God's name has happened? Blearily, Hew eyed the unwelcoming sight. Where was Marsaili and her family?

Dread settled low in Hew's empty stomach, twisting painfully. Surely Edmund hadn't followed her all the way across the Border, taking his revenge on all who lived here. But why else would the tower house appear abandoned?

He whirled, seeking the man who had dropped him at the gate, suddenly uncertain he wished to be here after all. But the cart dropped out of sight over a ridge, and Hew's old legs had no hope of catching up with the conveyance.

With trepidation, he trudged along the far side of the wall until he reached a small wooden gate set at an unobtrusive angle in the stone. He picked up a nearby stick and rapped on the square postern gate. With a squeak of rusty hinges, the narrow door reluctantly swung open.

Hew shivered, both from the cold and from anxious expectation. What lay beyond the gate? Friend or foe? Mayhap a ghost?

Fading sunlight fell across Hew's shoulders and landed a few inches inside the partially open door. Beyond was dark as the maw of hell. Hew swallowed nervously.

"Hullo?" His voice squeaked upward, changing the challenge to a question. Silence answered. Hew took a hesitant step backward, gathering himself to flee.

"Dinnae trip over yer feet." A feminine voice drifted through the opening.

Hew froze.

"Iseabal?" He strained to hear a response, half afraid of what he'd find if he opened the door farther.

A face appeared out of the gloom and Hew staggered back.

The lass sighed. "Come in, and dinnae act as if ye've seen a ghost. The only one here is tucked away in his shroud and not likely to harm anyone ever again."

≫≫≪≪

ISEABAL'S EYES TEARED at the sight of her sister's manservant. The strain of the past weeks had taken its toll, and she felt as if one kind word, even a kind look or a compassionate tilt of the head, would shatter her carefully constructed wall of indifference.

No one had dared answer the summons at the gate, but she'd heard the knock as she crossed the empty bailey on her return from the chapel.

Had Marsaili answered her missive? Though she'd begged her sister to travel with all haste, even with the hounds of hell behind her she could not have arrived this quickly. And, truth be told, after the way they'd parted nearly five years ago, Iseabal hadn't been certain her sister would read her letter, much less ride here and provide aid.

She peered past auld Hew but saw naught but the remnants of melting snow puddling on the muddy ground.

Her breath hitched. "Are ye alone? Is Marsaili not with ye? Or Flore?"

Surely Hew's sweet wife, who'd been the girls' nurse almost since their births twenty-three and more years ago, would have come to help. But Iseabal had heard from neither Hew nor Flore, or Marsaili for that matter, in the years since her sister's marriage to the English baron.

"Aye," Hew said. "I am alone." His eyes cut away, as if he was reluctant to offer a complete reply.

"Did ye get my letter?" she asked.

"Nae." He shook his grizzled head. "We've nae heard from ye these past years."

Panic slid icy fingers up Iseabal's spine. "Where is Marsaili?"

"We parted at an inn in England a month or more ago." His eyes rounded in distress. His hands gripped his elbows, hugging them to his skinny frame, reminding Iseabal of the cold.

Used to shouldering the troubles of others, Iseabal shifted her alarm into a gentle smile meant to reassure the old man.

"Dinnae fash. We will set things to rights. Come inside," she bade, motioning him through the gate. She closed and locked the door, pocketing the heavy metal key. Closing a hand over Hew's forearm, she halted his steps.

"I must warn ye," she said, capturing his attention. "Ye have noted the lack of soldiers on the wall." She waited for Hew's nod.

"I thought the keep was deserted," he admitted.

Weariness drew Iseabal's shoulders down as she remembered those who had escaped the keep no more than three days prior.

"It nearly is," she confessed. "Da went out reiving a fortnight back and returned with a pack of de Wolfe's men on his heels."

Hew's aged, parchment skin blanched.

"The keep held for a sennight or so, but the English tunneled beneath the wall to the north." She glanced over her shoulder as if she could see the damage from the postern gate. Thankfully she couldn't, but the thundering crash of the huge stones and the screams of women and dying men still rang in her ears.

"Da was struck by a portion of the wall, and when

he regained consciousness a few hours later, the English had already burned us out."

Iseabal wrung her hands. "There are only a few of us left. The men were either killed or taken away. They wanted to hang Da, but I begged them not to. Seeing him so close to death, their leader agreed." Tears stung the backs of her eyes, startling her when she thought she'd shoved her emotions deep inside.

"After stripping us of food and water and anything else they could manage, they left."

"Left ye alone?" Hew asked, indignant lines drawing his body up sharply. "With yer da dying? How many are left?"

"Six, counting me," Iseabal replied. "Though the others will likely bolt as soon as Da draws his last breath. I sent Marsaili a letter as soon as I could, hoping she would make the journey and find peace before Da passes." She peered past the auld man. "Why is she not with ye?"

Hew shook his head. "I lost her," he mourned.

Iseabal flinched. "Lost her?" she countered.

"Her husband died more than a month past. Her brother by marriage, a brute of a man who doesnae deserve to draw breath, kept her locked away, threatening to accuse her of Lord Ewan's death and petition the king for her arrest if she dinnae marry him."

"That's against the law!" Iseabal exclaimed.

Hew shrugged. "I dinnae ken the way of the English nobles, but if she'd agreed, attention wouldnae have been drawn to the marriage, legal or no'."

Iseabal gripped Hew's sleeve. "Where is she?"

"She escaped—me with her. Her horse went lame outside a small village south of the Border. 'Twas snowing somethin' fierce. She agreed we should wait out the storm at the inn, but when I came from securing rooms, she was gone."

Iseabal's hand flew to her throat. "She went on alone? Or do ye suspect foul play?"

"I dinnae ken," Hew mourned. "'Twas another conveyance in the yard when she left. I pray she dinnae fall afoul of those men."

"Who were they, Hew?" She tugged urgently on his arm. "Tell me!"

"The verra worst, milady," Hew said, his face twisted in fear and grief. "'Twas the rogue known as The Saint."

CHAPTER ONE

T HE MARCH WIND buffeted Iseabal, pulling black hair free from beneath the confining kerchief. Melted snow left its mark in icy puddles, an unusually cold winter that had kept Hew from making his way home immediately after he'd lost Marsaili far south of the Border.

People hurried past, most only nodding their condolences before mounting their waiting ponies and departing. Marcus Maxwell had not been a popular man.

Iseabal's focus shifted, her head bowed. There were few enough people at her father's funeral, and the crowd soon dispersed.

It has been more than a month by Hew's reckoning since he last saw Marsaili. Her heart sank. *Plenty of time for her to come home if she was able.* Had she run afoul of her evil brother by marriage or the man they called The Saint?

Where are ye, Marci?

She clutched her shawl about her shoulders.

"We should go inside, Iseabal," auld Hew muttered, his teeth clattering.

Instant remorse that she'd kept the loyal manservant standing out in the cold long after everyone else had left shot through her. "Pour yerself a mug of hot ale," she commanded, giving his shoulders a gentle shove to head him in the right direction. "I am right behind ye. And tell Aggie to finish packing. We will leave in the morn."

"With none to help ye here, her people at Friar Hill should be happy to take ye in," Hew noted. "They will take good care of yer laddie."

Iseabal nodded. Four-year-old Ewan was the joy of her life, though her da had threatened to disown her over her refusal to name the lad's father. Some secrets were meant to be kept.

With a spritely step indicating his relief, Hew led the way toward the keep and disappeared inside.

A whinny pulled Iseabal's startled gaze to the open gate. Mounted riders faced her, fanning out behind their leader, cloaks whipping in the biting wind. Iseabal stared, stomach roiling in alarm. A quick glance told her there were no others left in the yard. She faced them alone.

Dark eyes stared at her from bristling beards. The leader urged his horse forward, one hand on the hilt of his sword.

"I seek Marcus's daughter."

"I am she." Iseabal didn't bother to add there were two daughters. She had no idea where her sister was, and the information was unnecessary.

The man grunted. "He is dead?"

Her gaze cut to the mound of fresh soil and back. She bit back a stinging response.

"Aye. Took him nearly a sennight, but peace finally came."

"There are none others to mourn his passing?"

Iseabal glanced about the deserted yard. Memory of the attack turned her mourning into anger. "We were burned out, killed, scattered, some taken captive. A few lingered but left immediately after the funeral. Ye must've passed them on yer way in."

The man nodded and dismounted his horse. Iseabal took a step back. He tossed back his hood, his silvered hair bright.

"I am Albert Maxwell. Lord Maxwell's son."

Iseabal stared at him. Her father's brother. Or, half-brother. Lord Maxwell's legitimate heir. She'd never laid eyes on him, but she'd heard her father's disappointed rants and rambles often enough. Born on the wrong side of the blanket, Marcus would never win his father's approval. His elder half-brother, Albert, was all their father needed.

Albert Maxwell turned to his men and at his nod, they dismounted. A burly man, shorter than Albert and with the assured swagger of a bully, strode to his side. He planted his feet, folded his arms over his chest, and raked his gaze over Iseabal.

She shuddered, the degrading insolence of his gaze as forceful as if he'd actually touched her. The bully nodded once.

"She'll do."

THE HALL, SO eerily quiet after the English had attacked the keep, roared with curses, raucous laughter, and drunken witticisms. Iseabal sat ramrod straight in her chair, unable to do more than push her food about her platter as the noise swirled around her.

The burly man yanked the chair next to her from beneath the table and plopped his muscular form into its seat. His mug sloshed bitter ale onto the bare wooden table as he set it down with an unsteady thud.

"Shite! Damned table isnae level." He shoved the table's edge and laughed when more ale spilled. He swiveled to face Iseabal, a smirk twisting his lips.

Her skin crawled.

"I am James. Da has given me the keep," he announced. A corner of his mouth turned up as his eyes gleamed. "And everythin' in it."

Iseabal refused to answer and his leer fell into a scowl.

"We will wed."

She couldn't hide her shock. "That isnae possible. Ye are my cousin."

Albert turned to her from his seat on her other side.

"The keep is his. He may do as he wishes."

Despite herself, Iseabal's eyes widened and she slowly inspected Albert's son.

Beady eyes stared at her from beneath one thick brow. His nose, already veined and reddened with the tell-tale signs of indulgence, rested above a mustache ripe with bits of food, ale, and things Iseabal did not wish to examine.

I'd rather marry an Englishman.

Caution barely kept the words behind her teeth. She fisted her hands in her lap, her nails biting into her palms as she struggled to tame her racing heart.

"I will manage the keep for him." *For as long as it takes to hie away from here.* "But marrying him is out of the question. The church will not allow it."

James's glower dropped closer to anger, clearly a man unused to being denied.

"Then I will keep ye as my mistress," he growled.

Albert raised a hand. "No need." He graced Iseabal with an icy stare. "She has no family to contest the marriage." He leaned back in his seat and took a sip from his cup. "And the priest is easily swayed."

Hew appeared at her elbow, his wrinkled face creased further with concern. "My lady, Ewan is . . . ."

Iseabal didn't scold Hew for giving her a title when she had none, but understood his deference and subtle rebuke to the loathsome men at either side. She wondered how much he'd overheard. None of it mattered, however. She must see to Ewan before Albert or his son questioned her.

A child's wail pierced the rowdy commotion. At the base of the stairs, Aggie stooped, her charge tugging against her hold. The lad slipped free and darted across the room, dodging both her attempts to capture him, and the various legs, boots, benches, and bodies in his path.

Iseabal rose to her feet. Albert's fingers clamped over her wrist, tightening painfully. Bringing her hand up, she swept it across his arm and down, breaking his grip. She sent him a cold look then stepped to the side, folding Ewan against her as he catapulted into her skirts.

Albert's furious gaze promised retribution. He calmly picked up his cup and took another sip, his eyes riveted on the child in her arms.

"Who's bairn is that?"

Iseabal's heart raced. "Mine."

James burped loudly and sat up, peering at Ewan. He gaze swam to Iseabal. "Ye arenae a virgin?"

She leveled a steely glare at him and did not answer.

James glanced at his da, a scowl on his face. "I dinnae want a spoiled wife. I willnae take another man's bairn."

Albert stormed to his feet. "Ye will take her to wife."

James slumped back in his chair.

Albert spun to Iseabal. "Get rid of the brat."

SIMON DE BRETTESBY canted his head as Lady de Wylde laughed, her voice a pleasant trill cutting sweetly through the general clamor of the hall. The sound almost brought a smile to his face. Almost. His lord's new wife charmed everyone she met—including himself, though he was reluctant to admit it—but even her charms paled recently.

A failure of his own, not hers. Nothing seemed as bright as it had only a month earlier when Lord de Wylde, now Baron of Galewood, had given him the distinct honor of his own holding. North Hall was strategically placed between his home of Belwyck Castle and the Scottish Border, which is why, Lord de Wylde had explained, it needed Simon's leadership. Lord de Wylde, known along the Border as The Saint, had, it seemed, traded in his sword in anticipation of an enlarged family by late fall—and peace.

Simon shook his head at his friend's fanciful notion. Lord de Wylde was not infatuated enough with his new wife to imagine he'd never draw sword again.

His reputation and the Border were both too volatile for that. But he was still in the first throes of marriage, and diligent enough that his lady wife was rumored to be breeding. With years of fighting behind him—and the scars to prove it—The Saint sought peace.

Simon glanced about the room, newly reconstructed from the ruins of Friar's Hill—as it had been known during Scottish occupation. The Border was a fluid thing. What was once Scottish was now English, though who knew where the line would be in a year? Two?

Tonight he honored his liege lord and lady, welcoming them to his new hall. Colorful gowns and lithesome forms graced the chamber—a distinct difference from the past sennights when only a handful of dull-coated, rough-hewn knights and workmen had eaten at North Hall's tables. He heartily approved the change, though it appeared his month of roughing it without female companionship was not yet at an end.

"Times were simpler before The Saint accepted the title, eh Ellerton?"

Walter de Ellerton, his closest friend and now de Wylde's first in command, did not answer for the moment it took him to chew and swallow the chunk of roast pig he'd just placed in his mouth.

"'Tis quieter," he agreed, his words pensive and abbreviated as usual. Simon despaired of ever coaxing his friend into a deep philosophical discussion, or even light sardonic banter. No, Walter was too straightforward for such. But a better warrior or more loyal friend he'd never find.

"Battle is uncomplicated," Simon put forth, slouching on his bench—having relinquished his chair to de Wylde—pushing a piece of squash around on his trencher with the point of his knife. "Go here and fight. Go there and hold a castle." He paused, a thoughtful tilt to his head. "With no lingering long enough to break the ladies' hearts."

Walter grunted. "'Tis never worried ye before." He glanced from Lady Marsaili to Simon. "Looks like ye are wishing for a woman to do more than warm yer bed."

"Bah." Simon shoved his trencher across the table. "I like variety."

Walter grinned. "The women from Belwyck are familiar with yer reputation."

Simon snagged a piece of meat from Walter's tray and popped it into his mouth. "Mayhap ye are right," he grumbled around the pork. He swallowed. "The women who accompanied my lady greet me with sweet smiles and firm shakes of their lovely heads."

"They seek to be Lady of North Hall, not its master's bawd."

"Is that all they think about?" Simon tossed his knife to the table with a clatter. A group of young ladies at the far end of the table glanced up then tittered, heads clustered together like a flock of guinea hens. Simon eyed them, looking for the slight tilt of chin, the twinkle of an eye, anything to indicate one of the ladies would welcome his advances.

Nothing.

"Is it so wrong to share the master's bed?" he murmured, not really expecting Walter to answer.

"A woman doesn't wish a skirt full of bastards, Bretteby. Even the meanest among them wishes a husband who is faithful."

Simon shifted, placing a booted heel upon the bench. "Then why do ye not have women flocking to your side? Ye are strong, lacking in reputation as a lady's man, and not ill-favored—from a woman's standpoint."

To his surprise, Walter flushed. A dull red swept up

his neck and stained his weathered cheeks. "I do not have the funds to keep a wife," he replied, his voice low. "A woman isn't likely to see me as a worthy husband."

"Nonsense! Ye could have your pick of cottages in the keep and sport a new babe every year. The Saint isn't going to allow his commander's wife to lack in food or shelter." He clapped Walter on the shoulder as he rose. "I believe ye could have your pick of the young ladies here—if ye but showed an interest."

With sudden clarity, Simon caught the subtle drift of Walter's gaze. A young woman, her dark locks burnished copper and gold in the bright glare of torches, waited the tables.

"Ah, young Rosaline." Simon clucked his tongue sorrowfully. "I could inquire as to her preferences, though 'tis my understanding she is betrothed to one of the village lads."

Walter drew back, eyes wide. "Nae. I will not approach a woman who is spoken for."

Yet his gaze returned to Rosaline as she refilled mugs. She stiffened as a man's casual hand rested lightly on the curve of her buttock. Walter's knuckles whitened on his knife.

"Relax," Simon murmured. "My men know better than to force a wench."

Walter gave a single nod and wrenched his gaze away.

"We both should consider the benefits of a comely woman, even at the expense of installing her as a preferred bed partner for a time." Simon frowned. "Though I hesitate to give that much power to any who seek to rise above their rank."

"I could put forth a rumor ye are looking for a bride," Walter offered. "A lady for yer hall."

Dinner soured in Simon's belly. He leaned close to Walter's ear. "Ye do, and I will cut off that big nose of yers and feed it to the swine."

CHAPTER TWO

ISEABAL'S HEART RACED. A sour taste rose in the back of her mouth. Albert Maxwell and his son could force her to send Ewan away. Or have him killed.

She wanted to defy the order, but knew her son would be ripped from her arms if she did not appear frightened and obedient. She was most definitely frightened. Obedience, however, had never been her best attribute.

Aggie stepped hesitantly forward. "I will take him, m'lord."

Iseabal's gaze met Aggie's, and a bolt of understanding passed between them.

"I know of a family who'd be happy for a lad such as him. Dinnae fash." Aggie crossed the floor and knelt beside Ewan, her old knees creaking. "Come along, my wee *nacket*. Aggie will see to everything."

Ewan buried his face deeper into Iseabal's skirts. Firmly, gently, Iseabal pried his fingers from the cloth.

Holding his hands, she squatted before him.

"Go with Aggie, dearling. She is in charge of ye now." Certain her words had reached Albert, she leaned closer, inhaling the bairn's subtle scent as she whispered in his ear. "Dinnae fash. I will be upstairs with ye soon."

Ewan's body drooped in reluctance and she sent Aggie a fierce look. "Wait for me," she hissed.

Aggie gave a nearly imperceptible nod and gathered Ewan's unresisting form to her ample breast. Ewan gave Iseabal a final look of longing that tore her heart from her chest, then buried his face against Aggie's shoulder.

Knowing she'd never see him again if her half-formed plan did not work, Iseabal watched Ewan's golden head as Aggie climbed the stairs, child in her arms. She sank slowly into her chair. Numb. Unable to think.

"'Tis how things are done," Albert said, approval in his voice. "James simply doesnae wish an *ill-gotten* wean cluttering his hall when he has ye poppin' out bairns for him."

Iseabal suppressed another shudder and swallowed the urge to vomit. She mentally counted, giving Aggie time to get Ewan safely to her bedroom. The racket in the room washed over her in a blur of sound.

"Marcus may have been a bastard son, but he always knew where to find the best whisky!"

James's shout shook Iseabal from her focus as a cheer went up around the room. Wooden benches scraped along the floor as soldiers made way for two stout men who rolled a cask into the room. Two others followed. The sharp rap of a mallet rang as they opened the small barrels. Whisky was quickly ladled into mugs and passed about. The fumes, a heady blend of browned sugar, rum, and dried fruit, filled the room. With no small alarm, Iseabal hoped the stuff didn't ignite.

The whisky was quickly gone. Swilled by the swine in her hall. *Her* hall.

"Eaglesmuir is now mine!" James roared drunkenly.

Furious, Iseabal rose. James grabbed her arm, pulling himself to his feet. He stumbled forward and fell, shoving Iseabal to her back across the table, his belly atop hers. The odor of spilled whisky and cooling grease splashed over her. He sneered.

"Marcus's daughter is also mine." He ground his

pelvis into her, his cock mercifully flaccid after untold mugs of ale and whisky. A small bulge formed as he rocked back and forth.

"Get off me!" Iseabal shouted, battling back panic as her skirts rode up her legs.

James's grin widened and he planted his palms on either side of her head, locking his elbows to steady himself.

Stiffening her fingers, she drove them toward his eyes as hard as she could. James flinched his head, her strike landing on the bony rims rather than the globes themselves. She raked her nails down his cheeks, the leathery flesh tearing beneath the force. James screamed, his voice a high-pitched wail. He rolled to one side, his hands covering his face.

Iseabal quickly slid to the floor. Dropping to her knees, she dove beneath the table.

James came to his feet with a roar. A fist grasped her skirts, bruising her rear in the attempt to stop her. Iseabal rolled to her back and kicked her attacker. He released her and she scrambled backward on elbows, the broken ends of rushes digging into her wrists and palms. The bench behind her skidded across the floor as it was wrenched away. Hands grabbed her shoulders and hauled her to her feet.

Strands of hair straggling in her face, one sleeve ripped from its seams, she straightened, fury in every move. She met Albert's enraged look. He flung one hand to his side, blocking James from reaching her. James roared something, but her ears rang with the racing beat of her heart.

It couldn't have been complimentary.

She gulped a deep breath and her heart rate eased slightly.

"She's mine!" James tried to push past his da's arm. Albert silenced him with a look.

"Lock her in her room." Albert glanced about the hall, wariness replacing the shock on the men's faces. Some gripped the hilts of their swords, others braced a hand on a neighbor for stability.

Albert stepped around the table until his chest was only inches from Iseabal. Fury rolled off him in palpable waves, hot and dangerous.

"Ye will wed James in the morn. After yer vows, ye will belong to him."

SIMON ROLLED FROM the bed, his feet meeting the cold

boards of the lord's bedroom.

A rug or tapestry? Mayhap like those in bedrooms at Belwyck Castle? It had seemed a monumental waste of good weaving to toss the plush fabric onto the floor just to cushion one's feet, but after years campaigning with The Saint, sometimes in frigid weather, in conditions best described as crude, he was coming to believe the comforts of home should be just that— comfortable.

He glanced at the woman tangled in the blankets on the bed, her dark brown hair spilled in mysterious shadows across the white linen of the pillowcases. A memory flashed of silken hair of an even darker hue, so black it rippled with a blue sheen to her hips . . . .

He shook his head. Rising at dawn seemed to make him maudlin lately. And restless. Even more so since he'd taken over North Hall and found himself settling in as it's lord.

I do not want a wife! He stepped to the ewer. Pouring water into a bowl, he then splashed cold droplets over his face. Bracing. Manly. Frigid water dripped onto his belly and he flinched.

If this is what happens when one becomes lord of a holding, I prefer the stench of a battlefield and the awareness of being alive another day.

Kaily moaned softly and rolled to her back, breasts mounding beneath the thin blanket. Simon noted their shape appreciatively, recalling how they overflowed his hands. His cock twitched in mild interest, shocking Simon who'd considered climbing back into bed for an early morning tumble.

No more interest than that? Was he aging beyond the point of interest in women? The panicked thought skittered through his brain. How long before he grinned mindlessly at young women as they walked past without thought of bedding them?

He inhaled slowly. No, he'd had no difficulty last night bringing himself and Kaily to delicious heights of passion. Several times. Now sated, she simply did not interest him further.

Keeping that bit of information to himself, for he would surely welcome her back to his bed, if not this night, then another night soon, and did not wish to ruin her hopes of something more, he dressed and padded quietly out the door.

SIMON BLINKED AS his first-in-command halted next to him. Settling his forearms across the wide stone parapet wall, Garin tilted his head inquiringly. Simon stared over the land surrounding the keep, the rolling moorland giving way to forests, and beyond the woods, Solway Firth.

"Do ye recall the summer we brought Lord Maxwell's bastard son to heel?"

Simon clamped his mouth shut. Where did that come from? He'd meant to speak to Garin about the duty roster, not share his deepest thoughts.

Garin shrugged. "'Twas just after The Saint was injured and sent to recover at the monastery. We'd been recalled to Belwyck Castle where his eldest brother was lord at the time." He squinted as if stirring up the memory. "Ye were injured and we lost track of yer damn horse."

"I could not think straight after taking a blow to the head from that bearded Scot bastard," Simon admitted, though they'd been over this before.

"'Twas fortuitous, nae, a miracle ye discovered a place to hide until ye could manage to find yer way back across the Border." Garin slid his gaze to Simon, inviting him to reveal the truth of the matter. Silence stretched. "Though it took ye long enough."

Simon flipped a hand. "Bah. A handful of days. The

land is treacherous north of the Border."

"The Scots are treacherous, as well. 'Twould have been easier if ye'd had help."

Simon hesitated. He'd told only Walter the truth of his injury. Of the sweet Scottish lass who'd hidden him when he'd stumbled from the woods after being thrown from his horse—incurring a second bump to his already damaged head.

Gentle fingers had stroked his stubbled cheek, pink lips murmured soothing words. Her skin glowed, the palest he'd ever seen, yet its rosy tint warmed him to his toes.

So had the passion she'd shared with him almost a sennight later when he was in his right mind and he'd loved her beneath a summer moon.

Mayhap he hadn't been in his right mind. She'd been wise for her years, solemn. He'd wanted to tease a smile onto her lips, ease the fierce denial which had come over her when it was clearly time for him to leave. It had been madness to seduce the Scottish lass. Madness he only rarely allowed himself to remember. Yet her memory had risen more and more lately.

She'd likely married long ago, with a passel of brats at her heels. A knot twisted in his gut to think of her in another's arms, though he had no claim on her—other than the privilege of sharing her first encounter, willingly and passionately.

"The Saint will be sending more men to help guard the keep. He approves of the restoration we've done. North Hall will be an important buffer between Belwyck and the Border." Simon halted, aware he was mouthing words Lord de Wylde had said only two days earlier.

"I will determine their skills and adjust our duty roster accordingly," Garin replied with no notice made to Simon's topic change.

"I need a steward, someone who can take charge of the daily bookkeeping. Mayhap help find people to rebuild the village." He nodded to a small cluster of ramshackle cottages nestled beneath the protective wing of North Hall's eastern wall. A little-used road ran roughly from the southeast, continuing in a north-west route to the Solway Firth where fishing and shipping were the predominant trades. A few cattle who'd survived the handful of years since the English had taken the land from the Scots grazed nearby, sheltering in the cottages.

"I can send a couple of men around to the nearby

villages. Mayhap offer the housing free in exchange for work. And have them keep an eye out for a likely steward, though one of our own from The Saint might be preferable."

"Aye. I'll take it up with him." He grunted. "My own keep. I scarcely know where to go from here."

Garin slapped the top of the stone wall lightly. "Ye are doing well. Ye have built this from abandoned shell to comfortable keep. I'll get the workers started on reinforcing the wall—considering the Scots likely still consider it theirs and will come calling soon—and often. I predict the land will support us by next summer. Mayhap this one if we can get gardens planted and add to the cattle. Possibly sheep, as well."

"Yes. Much left to do."

Garin turned to go, then glanced over his shoulder. "And a lady to help run the place," he added, a sly grin on his face. Simon merely nodded, memories overtaking him once again.

Silken black hair. Piercingly green eyes. The scent of lavender and peat. Whispered words he'd meant at the time.

"I will remember ye always, my dove. My heart."

CHAPTER THREE

ONE OF ALBERT'S soldiers squeezed Iseabal's buttock before another shoved her into her room. She stumbled two steps before whirling, fists clenched. The two comrades laughed and slammed the door in her face, their bawdy comments muffled behind the solid portal.

Iseabal did not waste time rubbing her aching shoulder or dusting the lingering sensation from her backside. Both were a reminder that the men who now occupied Eaglesmuir had no qualms about abusing a woman. Their actions spoke loudly of what her life would become should she remain.

Escape had never been more urgent.

A key turned in the lock and she resisted the urge to kick the door in frustration. With a deep breath, she turned her gaze to the darkest corner of the room where a large chest stood several feet from the wall.

"Aggie?"

The auld nurse rose from behind the chest, Ewan's hand tucked firmly in hers. Ewan whimpered and rubbed his eyes, clearly on the verge of an exhausted tantrum. Iseabal hurried to him, enveloping him in a hug before placing him on the bed beneath the covers where he curled into a ball and dropped instantly into sleep.

Iseabal dropped a kiss to his cheek and tucked the blanket beneath his chin then turned to Aggie.

"Have ye packed his things?"

"Aye, and yers as well." She lifted her shoulders in puzzlement. "I heard the key turn in the lock. How will we leave?"

"I am counting on Hew to help us. He saw what happened and must know he'll need a key to get in. We must wait until the men are drunk enough they willnae hear us escape."

"If they've discovered yer da's cache of whisky, that mayn't take long," Aggie observed drily.

Iseabal glanced at Ewan, who slept fitfully, then back to Aggie. "I must tell ye, 'tis Da's half-brother, Albert, and his son, James, who have taken Eaglesmuir. To keep things in the family, Albert has decreed I wed James on the morrow."

She shook her head as Aggie reared back, eyes wide, a hand to her breast. "I willnae be here for the wedding. I must take Ewan and flee. Ye and Hew are to make yer own decisions, though ye will be most welcome should ye decide to join us."

"Och! I willnae leave yer side, my lamb. 'Twould only be a matter of time before I lost my patience with the lot of 'em here. They're a *radgie* group, make no mistake. Not fit company for a woman, despite my years."

Iseabal's shoulders relaxed and she patted the woman's hand. "Thank ye, Aggie. Ye dinnae know what this means to me."

Aggie smiled. "We'll go to Friar's Hill as we discussed these past sennights. That lot," she nodded toward the door, "willnae know of our plans, so we'll be safe enough there. My kin are good folk and will take us in."

"Ye have been verra kind to Ewan and me," Iseabal said, perilously close to tears. She shook her head. There was simply no time to waste on sentiment. She'd meant to be on her way in a day or two anyway. There'd been no sense in lingering once her da was in his grave. Someone who had the skills to repair the keep would take it sooner or later, but she'd expected to leave of her own accord, not chased from her home by a lecherous brute.

That was *before* Maxwell and his son arrived and forced her to flee. Leaving Eaglesmuir in the hands of the likes of James Maxwell infuriated her, drove her loss deep within as if on the point of a sword. She managed a brave smile for Aggie's sake.

"Then, let us finish preparations and hope Hew is able to locate a key."

⋙✦⋘

"A REPORT FROM the Border, my lord." The young man placed a packet on the desk at Simon's direction. He waited patiently as Simon perused the thin, worn parchment, unrolling it as he read. After a moment, Simon nodded dismissal and the messenger pivoted sharply on his heel and marched from the room.

Garin strode past the young man and paused before Simon's desk. Simon glanced up then motioned vaguely to a chair. Gavin sat, but remained silent until Simon gave him his full attention.

"I am certain my news is what ye just read, but it bears repeating. The Maxwells have been rather active lately."

Simon glanced at the document on his desk. "I've no reports of a border crossing. A holding near Lockardebi has exchanged hands. The old lord died, I believe."

"He wasn't old. Stubborn, unprincipled, a right bastard at times. He died because he decided reiving cattle from an English nobleman some miles from here would be a notch on his belt. Unfortunately for him, there was a contingent of de Wolfe soldiers in the area who immediately gave chase. He holed up in his keep and withstood a two-day siege, but they at last were overtaken. Marcus Maxwell was mortally wounded when a portion of the wall fell on him."

"Is it your opinion the Maxwells will demand retribution?" The notion seemed far-fetched to Simon, for this Marcus had willingly created the events that led to his death, but he knew the Scots to be a hot-headed lot, always spoiling for a fight.

"They can scarcely cry foul, can they?" Gavin asked with a tilt of his head. "Did the English vengeance for stolen cattle go too far? 'Tis certainly open for debate. Marcus Maxwell was Lord Maxwell's bastard son. He has a legitimate heir and grandson to secure the line. 'Tis rumored Marcus was given the small keep at Eaglesmuir and then left to succeed or fail on his own terms. He received little enough support from his father beyond that."

"Ah, but where family may be allowed to deride the bastard, they are likely to rally kith and kin to his side if outsiders do so." The corner of Simon's mouth tilted up. "'Tis well we keep watch on the Maxwells. Diligence may save us more than a bit of trouble."

Garin rose to his feet. "I will set a patrol. 'Twill leave us short-handed at the wall for a few days until Lord de Wylde's men arrive, but mayhap worth the extra labor."

Simon stretched then stood. "I will be happy to lend a hand. I grow weary of sitting behind this desk."

"As ye will. I referred to reinforcing the wall, which a few soldiers had volunteered to assist with. There has been no activity of late and they seek work to relieve the boredom."

Simon shrugged. "Not to mention we will be safer once the fortification is complete. I will at least take my turn upon the wall, and mayhap heft a few stones with the men. I am certain it could prove interesting."

>>>><<<<

THE CANDLES HAD burned to stubs. Nervous energy consumed Iseabal and she paced the floor, scarcely able to restrain from testing the door latch with each passing.

"Ye will wear yerself out, lamb, if ye dinnae stop." Aggie, seated on a chair pulled next to the bed, patted the mattress edge. "Come sit a spell."

Knowing Aggie was right, Iseabal abandoned her vigil and slid onto the bed next to Ewan. She brushed back a hank of his golden hair, so different from her own black locks, and with even more curl. Like his father.

Fortunately, Ewan's features were all Maxwell. Her green eyes in a face beginning to lose its baby softness. At times she could see her sister Marsaili's straight nose, or her da's lowering brow when Ewan was vexed. None of the slender features of his da, whose looks had run more angelic than those of a warrior.

Her worry ebbed. She had loved her English warrior. She had defied her da's orders about wounded enemy soldiers and hidden him away in a tiny abandoned shepherd's hut while she nursed him back to health. And, when he was about to walk away, she'd given him her heart—and her virtue.

Iseabal glanced up at the timid knock at the door. Certain there wasn't a lout below stairs capable of anything softer than a crashing thud or a bellow, she hurried to the portal and leaned against the wood.

"Hew?"

"Aye. May I come in?"

"If ye have a key," she replied drily. To her relief, the scrape of metal proved he'd been successful. Aggie hurried across the room as Iseabal disengaged the latch. Auld Hew hesitated in the doorway. With a shrug, he stepped into the room, his rheumy gaze taking in the few amenities in the stark chamber.

"I've naught been in a lady's quarters afore," he avowed.

"I am grateful to see ye," Iseabal said in an attempt to redirect his attention. "Tell me what news in the hall."

He straightened as much as his arthritic frame would allow. "There's naught a man down there who can hold his whisky," he scoffed. "Why, yer da . . . ."

"My *Da* isnae here," Iseabal reminded him impatiently. *And is the reason I am in this mess.*

She waved a hand. "Is it time? What are our chances of escape?"

"Och, they're fair *fuddelt*, yon Maxwells are. A whole English garrison could pass through the hall and naught a man would know of it." He winked and held up the heavy key. "'Tis why I had nae trouble fetchin' this wee bit o' iron."

Iseabal patted Hew's shoulder then turned to Aggie. "Gather the bags. We daren't try for horses. Even if the guards at the stable are drunk as well, the animals cannae be trusted to be silent. The snow is past and though we'll only travel at night, the days look to be fair enough for our trek to Friar's Hill."

"It shouldnae take us more than two nights' travel," Aggie assured her. "Though I havenae been there in several years—why, not since wee Ewan was born. I dinnae think we will be on the road longer than that."

"Good. We will slip away as quickly as possible."

She drew her cloak over her shoulders. Placing the hood over her head, she pulled the edge low over her face. She looped a thong over her belt, the leather flagon attached filled with watered ale. Her small personal bag attached to the other side of her belt. Aggie checked the pack of oatcakes and cheese, then tightened the drawstring neck and draped it over her shoulders. Hew hefted a pack of Ewan's belongings, the wooden horse crafted by a young soldier for the lad's first birthday clanking softly against the ship Ewan had stuffed into the pack earlier in the day.

Iseabal shot Hew a look of warning, though she knew he was unlikely to remove a toy the lad loved. He'd been smitten with Ewan since arriving at the keep three days earlier.

While Hew stuffed a scrap of linen inside his pack to silence the toys, Iseabal gently wrapped Ewan in as many blankets as she could, making a sling of the last, and cuddled him in her arms. With a nod, she sent Hew to the door. He put an ear to the panel and listened before opening it carefully. Faint snores reached their ears, but no one challenged them as they silently crept down the stairs.

Iseabal directed them through the kitchen and over the crumbled garden wall. The sheep fold beyond the garden had fared slightly better, though the English had taken all of the animals when they retreated over the Border. The shepherd's dog, unimaginatively named Shep, had protected his flock until a soldier had cracked him over the head, leaving him in the yard as the sheep dashed through the gate, wobbly new lambs at their sides.

Lacking a sheep dog, Iseabal could only imagine the havoc of herding the animals across the Border. Shep had been unable to stand for two days, and still listed to the right like a ship crabbing into the wind. Ewan had helped her nurse the dog back to health, and Shep had become attached to the lad. It was a blessing the dog hadn't been in the keep when the Maxwells had arrived. It was likely the dog would have sustained further injury at their hands.

Shep met them at the entrance to the fold, white-tipped tail swaying gently. Iseabal patted her skirt in invitation for him to join them, and he licked her hand then quietly paced alongside. Slipping through the postern gate no one had bothered to fix, they faded into the night.

CHAPTER FOUR

J AMES MAXWELL SLAMMED his fist on the table, wincing at the dull thud that echoed in his whisky befuddled brain. "I want her found! Dinnae tell me no one knows where she is. What about that nursemaid?" He rubbed the scabs streaking down his cheeks.

"Ye sent the auld woman and the brat away," Thom, his long-time friend, reminded him. His slim, gangly body rarely seemed to be affected by exercise or alcohol, and his bright eyes infuriated James this morning.

"Where is Iseabal?" His voice rose as he slowly turned his head, viewing the nearly empty room with not a female in sight. A few men huddled over their morning ale, food platters untouched.

Damn, Marcus's whisky carries a bite.

He'd been drunk before, but this took the experience to new heights. His head ached, his eyes were blurry, his tongue swollen and dry. His stomach felt both empty and full, recoiling at the thought of food. His hands didn't seem to work quite right, either, he noted, as he reached for a cup that ever seemed just out of reach.

Someone banged a mug next to his fist, scraping the rough edge along the back of his hand before it landed on the poorly sanded plank. James drew back, unable to process this new pain of skinned and bruised flesh.

"Wha . . .?"

"Shut yer mouth, or I'll do it for ye."

His da's fierce undertone cut through the lingering fog in James's brain, inspiring him to silence. He hunched his shoulders forward and slipped his aching hand into his lap.

"Did ye nae set a guard at her door?" Albert asked, anger sparking through his words.

"My men locked it," James whined. "She shouldnae have escaped."

"Have ye searched the keep? Are there any horses missing?" Albert clapped a heavy hand on James's shoulder. "Do not tell me the guards at the gate were drunk as well. By God, I've never seen such a slip-shod mess."

James shrugged off his da's grip. "'Twas a celebration. But I only sent them a single cask of whisky."

"Idiot. Ye *cannae* be my son," Albert growled. "Ye dinnae deserve a holding of yer own if ye cannae keep one lass in her room for the night. When did ye discover she was missing?"

James sucked his front teeth, pulling moisture into his mouth. "I ordered Thom to bring the wench to me not an hour ago. I wanted to be certain she was ready to obey me and come before the priest. She doesnae fear me properly." He touched his face, scabs tender beneath his fingertips. His anger rose.

Albert shook his head, his pinched lips white along the edges. His glare sent James's belligerence back into hiding. He sulked.

"I want a report," Albert shouted, whirling to address the room. The men in the hall glanced up.

"I want to know if any horses are missing. If anyone has seen *James's bride*." He bit out the last two words through gritted teeth.

"And bring me the guards on duty at the gate last night."

ISEABAL RELUCTANTLY HANDED Ewan's sleeping form to Hew. The lad had walked until he gave out, struggling to keep up with the pace the adults set. Iseabal pushed to keep them going, giving only faint heed to Aggie's and Hew's advanced ages, knowing the more distance between them and Eaglesmuir, the better their chances of escape. Hew was wiry and willing to carry his share of the burdens, but she didn't expect his strength to last much longer. She knew carrying the four-year-old would sap the old man's energy quicker than the long hours they'd been on the run. But Hew had insisted and her back ached from the strain.

Dawn pearled the sky and they would soon be forced to find a place to hide for the day. Iseabal gathered Aggie and Hew to her side as they approached the village of Annan, near the Solway Firth.

"It willnae be long before our escape is discovered. Whether they will suspect we left together or not, I couldnae say." She nodded to Aggie. "Ye were ordered to remove Ewan from the keep, so I'd like to doubt they will seek an auld woman and a lad." She looked at Hew. "The two of us are another matter. I believe we can find sanctuary at the Church of Annan. Leave Ewan with me and take a handful of coins. Find food and keep yer ears open."

Iseabal's gaze slipped to the sight of her son's golden curls ruffled above the blanket that framed his head. It was a gamble to enter the village, but its size would help to hide them. The easier path across the Border—should the Maxwell soldiers think to follow her south—was through Gretna Green, some miles to their east.

Let them waste their time seeking us there.

The difficult part of their journey would be finding passage across the firth. The eagle eyes of the ferry men missed nothing. A bribe would be enough to set James's men on their trail. One more night should see them within welcoming arms. They'd already covered more ground than she'd dared hope. Reaching Annan was a boon.

Iseabal took Ewan from Hew before they reached Annan. They stumbled, weary-footed and hungry, into the village, timing their entry so they mingled with the early morning bustle of merchants and farmers. Shep whined as a flock of sheep hustled past, two gaunt collies, bellies low to the ground, maneuvering their silly, bleating charges through the throngs of people, animals, and wagons.

The church, rosy stone aglow in the sun's early rays, appeared warm and welcoming. Hew beckoned to Shep and they shambled down the street in search of a vendor for food to break their fast, while Iseabal and Aggie entered the small church.

An elderly woman, a heavy shawl over her shoulders, approached them. Her eyes, an unusual pale blue, peered from a wrinkled face. Her round body was swathed in a multitude of muted colors of brown, blue, and green, and her head, hair pinned up in an untidy nest, barely reached Iseabal's shoulder. She stopped before them, head tilted bird-like to one side.

"I am Ava. How may we comfort ye this bright morn?" she asked, her chipper voice adding to Iseabal's fanciful notion of a bird.

"We travel to visit kin across the firth," Iseabal answered. "I've been reassured the Border is quiet."

"Hee! When is the Border ever quiet, lass?" Ava's eyes twinkled. "Have ye no escort? Traveling alone isnae wise."

"The men have gone in search of food," Iseabal replied, stretching the truth slightly. "My lad is weary and I thought this to be a quiet spot to rest a bit."

"Och, what a bonny lad!" the woman chirped,

stepping closer to peer at Ewan's golden curls. "Mustn't let the laddie miss his nap. I've a wee room just over there where the three of ye may bide a while." She stepped down the aisle and led Iseabal and Aggie to a tiny room. Iseabal couldn't guess its use, though it smelled vaguely of flowers. A bench stood along one wall.

"I'll pull this door to and ye'll not be bothered by the comings and goings later. Easter is but a fortnight away and there will be lasses in to clean from top to bottom. I'll make certain they dinnae disturb ye."

"I'm verra grateful," Iseabal replied. She remembered the dreadful sound of a turned key in her bedroom door's lock, and hesitated to be closed inside this small room. "Aggie will wait outside for our food."

Silence filled the church once Ava retreated. Iseabal nudged the door to the room open a hand's breadth or more. She was uneasy to have the door open completely, but left it ajar enough to give her a view of the church yet still maintain a fair degree of privacy.

Dust motes danced on beams of light shimmering through tall, slender windows, the rays warming the stone floor. Ewan stirred and Iseabal crooned softly, pushing the blanket from his head as he peered sleepily around the small room.

"I'm hungry."

Iseabal smiled. "Of course ye are, my wee *nacket*. Hew has gone to fetch some food, but I have a bit for ye in the meantime." She sat Ewan on the bench and handed him a bannock. He accepted it and nibbled slowly, still not fully awake. He finished the paltry sustenance and Iseabal offered him a sip of watered ale. With a sigh, he magically changed from drowsy wean to wide-awake lad. Hopping down, he crept to the door and peered into the church then back to his ma.

"Where are we?"

"We are almost halfway to the place Aggie lived when she was a lass. Do ye remember the name?"

Ewan scrunched his face in thought. He shook his head then brightened. "Friar's Hill!" He grinned.

"Verra good! And I thought ye werenae listening," Iseabal teased.

Ewan peered around the door again. "Are we hiding so the bad men won't find us?"

Iseabal's heart squeezed painfully. He'd lived the past month surrounded by battle and its dreadful aftermath. She wondered how much he'd seen and heard the night before.

"The men who arrived yesterday werenae verra nice," she offered gently.

Ewan looked over his shoulder, his nose wrinkled. "They smelled bad."

"Aye, they did."

"And they were noisy. They used their ugly voices." He raised his hands, holding them far apart. "*Big* voices."

Iseabal sighed. "Aye. Ye are right. All the more reason to make a new home at Friar's Hill with Aggie and Hew."

"My da would've made them leave." Ewan nodded assertively.

Iseabal raised an eyebrow. He'd been inquisitive about his father lately, likely a result of the lads he played with, sons of soldiers. "Yer da would have protected us. Let us find a privy then see what Aggie has for us to eat."

⇒⇒⇒⇐⇐⇐

SIMON WIPED HIS brow with the back of a hand. The spring air was cool, but hard work in the sun beaded sweat on his brow. A trickle made its way down his back beneath his tunic. He hunched his shoulders, the strain of lifting heavy rocks and setting them in place stressing muscles sword play didn't. The wall repairs were coming along nicely, and it pleased him to assist with the effort.

He was also pleased to see the sun dipping below the horizon. Supper and bed beckoned.

A full belly and a long day's work put him into a pensive mood. The prior night's mention of Clan Maxwell drew his memories together, back to the day five years ago when he'd led a retaliatory raid on Scots reivers.

Pulling himself onto his horse inch by painful inch after receiving a staggering blow from a burly Scot that had knocked him to the ground. Barely able to hold himself in the saddle as his horse wandered off into the night. Waking to find himself in heaven. Or it would have been if the pain in his head had not served to convince him he'd landed in hell.

The face above him, blurred and wavering, had nonetheless spoke to him in a gentle Scottish burr, tender hands placing cool cloths on his throbbing head. Two days later, as his headache abated and he discovered he'd truly been rescued by an angel, he decided he'd landed somewhere much nicer than what likely awaited him at the end of his days.

She'd tended him well, his Scottish lass. And he remembered her and the days that followed with immense fondness. Like the memory of an excellent, aged Oloroso sherry, redolent with the aroma of walnuts and raisins. Rich, multi-layered, yet elusive.

"Word from the Border." Garin sat in the chair next to Simon at his nod. "The Maxwells appear to be up to something. Robert brought a load of fish from the wharf at Bowness this eve, and heard of a commotion a few miles north of the firth. It seems the Scots are brewing some sort of mischief."

"I would counter with the question, when are they not brewing mischief, except . . . ." Simon frowned. He couldn't quite put his finger on the source of his unease. Perhaps it was the lack of soldiers in a keep that was still vulnerable. The men promised to him by The Saint, Lord de Wylde, would arrive in the next day or two. He would keep extra patrols until then, ensuring warning before anyone drew close enough to North Hall to attack.

"Widen the patrols. Ensure the line of communication is easily accessible. We must finish the wall's repairs as quickly as possible."

"The men understand the urgency. They will resume the work at dawn."

Simon rubbed his chin. "Have we missed anything?"

"I will see to it the brush we've cleared from around the wall is burned. Once the wall is completed, we can widen the cleared area around the keep. Use the trees to help rebuild the village."

"We will soon be able to defend the village. It will then grow."

Garin nodded. "There are a few families, a rather hardy sort of mixed Scots and English blood. It appears to take more than English occupation to roust them from their cottages."

"I'd like to see the village flourish once again. But they must accept an Englishman as their lord."

"'Tis not the first time North Hall has had an English lord."

"No. But it was in Scottish hands for many years."

"I believe the tendency is to accept the power as it arises. In the villagers' view, what is English today, could very well be Scottish tomorrow."

Simon sent his commander a stern look. "I do not intend to lose my keep to Scottish marauders. Not now. Not ever."

CHAPTER FIVE

T WO BURLY FISHERMEN dragged the boat ashore, its hull scraping along the thick mud and half-submerged flat rocks. Iseabal, Hew, and Aggie carefully disembarked, mindful of the mud sucking at their boots, Ewan in Iseabal's arms. Shep leapt over the rail, landing lightly on the rocks and setting off at a brisk pace up the shoreline.

The birlinn reeked of fish, old wood, and sun-dried nets, but Ewan had been enchanted with the trip across the firth and proved reluctant to leave. After his day of forced inactivity in the church, he'd been more than ready to take on a walk to the shore and the excitement of boarding the boat. Barnacle geese flew overhead, much to his delight, in choruses of honks and yaps, to settle in reeds and other hiding places for the night.

The fishermen pushed their craft back into the water then climbed aboard and headed home across the firth, their pockets a little richer for their trouble.

Iseabal handed Ewan a piece of dried fish as they hurried along the path to the village. Heads down to avoid arousing attention, they quickly made their way through the narrow streets and into the countryside as shadows lengthened and nighttime turned their world into shades of black and gray and the white glow of the moon.

They continued along the road, though Iseabal would have preferred to avoid the well-traveled route. Boggy land crept past the edges of the occasional burn, snaring the unwary and providing difficult footing even for daylight travelers. Her ears stretched beyond the soft tread of boots on the packed earthen road, above Ewan's chatter and Hew's baritone responses.

The constant strain exhausted her. Her heart raced, her eyes darted to every shadow, every puddle of pale moonlight. Moors and farmland gave way to woods and gently rolling hills. Night birds soared overhead. Small, quick-footed creatures scurried on either side of the road.

Ewan's energy waned and Iseabal called for a brief halt. Aggie passed bannocks around, followed by the flagon Iseabal had refilled in Annan. Ewan whined, unused to the late hour and constant travel. Shep curled at their feet, content with his share of the slim rations. Ewan dug his fingers into Shep's thick coat and the dog scooted closer.

"There, there, sweeting," Aggie crooned, pulling Ewan into her lap. She patted his golden curls and he rested his head on her shoulder. "Let Aggie tell ye about yer new home. A fair place it is, with deer in the woods and wild geese overhead."

"Like the ones we saw on the boat?" Ewan murmured.

"Aye. And others." She rocked him gently. "And a keep on the hill much like Eaglesmuir, with a wee burn that runs past and to the village."

"Can I sail boats on it?" He kicked his boot at a rock near Aggie's hip.

"Ye can sail boats, mayhap even learn to swim in the deeper parts—but only with yer ma or me along with ye."

"Can Hew come?" he asked, pausing to peer over his shoulder at the old man.

"I dinnae know how to swim," Hew admitted.

"I've a nephew or two who can teach ye," Aggie said. "Hew will have other duties."

"I cannae wait to start our new life," Iseabal sighed.

"Ye are a godsend, Aggie."

"Dinnae fash, my lamb. The folk at Friar's Hill are fine people, and 'twill be good to rest my bones among kin. Not like the *wratches* back at Eaglesmuir, though yer da doesnae appear to have fallen far from his family tree."

"No. He often mourned not being accepted into the family. But it seems he fit the mold well."

"We're well-shed of them now. I'll rest easier when ye've a nice young man on yer arm and a bairn or two to give wee Ewan some competition."

Not certain whether to laugh or shudder at Aggie's fond hopes, Iseabal shook her head.

"How far do ye think we are?"

"Och, not far. Let's rest a wee bit longer. We pushed verra hard last night so none would find our trail, and I believe Hew's auld bones are a bit knack-ered still."

"I'm ready to go again as soon as ye are, auld wom-an," Hew blustered. "I willnae hold ye back."

Iseabal remembered how long it had taken him to reach Eaglesmuir after he'd *lost* Marsaili. His years did not rest so kindly on him as in days past. Mayhap a brief rest—to give Ewan a bit more time—would be for the best.

Thinking of Marsaili gave Iseabal pause. Finding her sister was the next step to accomplish once she was assured of their acceptance at Friar's Hill. Aggie's reassurances did much to soothe her worries, but life had become too unpredictable for her to believe fully until she could see the outcome for herself.

She also remembered how heavy Ewan had become. Carrying his sleeping body was no easy task, and her back and shoulders ached at the thought. This side of the firth felt safer, and with much of their travel past, what could it hurt to linger until Ewan woke from his nap?

⠀⠀⠀⠀⠀⠀⠀⠀⠀⠀⠀⠀⠀⠀⠀⠀⠀⠀⠀⠀>>>><<<<

JAMES GLARED ABOUT the hall, his gaze hindered by the smoky haze from a partially-blocked chimney, an eye that still had not regained its full function after Iseabal's assault—and a final draught of Marcus's fine whisky. His men lounged about the hall, a few already snoring though the sun had scarcely set. His da had left him twenty soldiers—only twenty—to manage the keep. It wasn't enough. Most were lads with whom he'd grown up, with shared tales of debauchery and vice between them. Only a few were seasoned warriors.

I willnae leave good men subject to yer ineptitude, James. Learn to lead, not bully. Enlarge yer holdings under yer own mettle. Come speak with me when ye've wed, have a bairn on the way, and this keep under control.

Albert had stormed from the hall, summoned his horse, and galloped away, taking nearly thirty of the best warriors Clan Maxwell boasted.

James threw his mug at the fireplace. Its contents hissed on the dark embers beneath the flames and the pottery shattered against the stone.

"I want . . . ." What *did* he want?

"I want more." He paused. "Land. Tenants. I want men to repair the keep."

"Ye need money, James," Thom replied. "We arenae so good at making money."

"How will I hire masons if I must pay them?" James scowled. "What *are* we good at?"

Thom shrugged. "Fightin'. Swivin'."

"There's none here to fight. The English retreated and we have Johnstones and Carlisles on our borders. And there's naught a lass left here to swive."

Thom stared into his mug. "It wouldnae do to reive

from our neighbors. We cannae risk an ongoing feud just now." He glanced up, his stare remarkably clear after the whisky he'd consumed. "We'll need to ride south of the firth."

Thom's words filled James with purpose. He and his men *were* good at reiving. And the village of Friar's Hill, family to a few Maxwells as well as Murrays and the occasional Johnstone, had been routed by the English nearly two years back, with none to avenge them. In fact, 'twas only proper to replace the sheep the English had stolen from Eaglesmuir with others reived from an English holding. One too far away to make an ongoing feud practical.

"Is Friar's Hill still standing? I've heard naught about them this past year and more."

Thom nodded. "As well as I know. When the de Wylde brothers took the land, none dared ride against them. Since they died, there's only the one brother who's spent the past twelvemonth recovering from an injury. 'Tis said he's a cripple."

James's head cleared abruptly. "The Saint?"

"Naught in a name if ye arenae man enough to back it up."

"He is feared all along the Border!" James shuddered. Reiving was one thing—a fine, honorable thing—but tweaking the ire of The Saint?

"Are ye certain he is crippled? How far is Friar's Hill from his keep?"

Thom thought for a moment. "He was crippled when he arrived at Belwyck a month or so ago, according to rumor. I havenae heard since. Friar's Hill is a half-day's easy ride from there, but if we time it right, we'll grab the sheep and be gone before The Saint knows we've been there."

It seemed easy enough. Ride south, slip into Friar's Hill before dawn, steal a few sheep, and be back across the firth before anyone gave chase.

His mood soured again. He'd been searching all day—well, most of it, anyway—for his runaway bride. When he wasn't arguing with his da or eating. He'd needed a lot of sustenance for the job ahead. And the food they'd brought with them was all but gone, and no one had stepped forward as cook for the keep.

"I want to find Iseabal." He shoved Thom's mug across the table. "She should be forced to come back and care for me. This keep needs a woman!"

"This keep needs a lot of women," Thom agreed. "I can think of a few duties I dinnae wish handed over to the likes of Johnnie." He waggled a hand at the red-haired man across the room, his bulk weighing in a bit over twenty stone. "Though he should prove a dab hand as cook if ye judge such things by a man's girth."

"Johnnie could burn water," James groused. "'Tis eatin' he does best." He pounded his fist on the table. "I want a woman!"

"Then raid the English. Prove ye are a Scot worth yer mettle. Yer da doesnae believe ye are capable of such a task, and yer wife-to-be doesnae appear to value ye, either." Thom leaned close. "Bring back the fattest sheep, show the manner of man ye are, and the bonniest lasses will follow."

"They will respect me for my reiving prowess." James's words were firm.

"Aye." Thom lifted his mug. "To reiving!" he shouted.

The room roared. "Reiving!"

"Grab yer hoods and saddle yer horses! This night, we ride to the Border!"

⟫⟫⟫⟪⟪⟪

SIMON COULDN'T SLEEP. Restless and tired was no way to spend the night, and even Kaily's charms had failed to keep him in his bed. He paced slowly along the parapet, nodding to the soldiers as he passed. The full moon overhead gave the creatures of the night full rein over the field and woods. A stag, his antlers large enough to be seen at a distance, slowly stalked the rise beyond the burn. A hunting bird soared soundlessly overhead, the shadow of his wings sweeping across the moon-bright ground.

Simon's tension eased as he viewed the land surrounding the keep. The wall was repaired, though he would begin a larger, wider wall as soon as workmen could be found. Grass beginning to green again as the weather warmed, swept out from the wall, a swath of open land that allowed no one to hide.

"We could ride to the village if ye cannot sleep." Garin noted, appearing on the wall.

"Have cook set aside something for us to take with us. I believe I will fare better with a horse beneath me and a purpose ahead than brooding over the walls."

"The sun will be up anon. I will ready a dozen men to ride with us."

"Don't make us appear too fierce." Simon smiled. "Firm, capable, but not so fierce workers will not dare return with us."

Garin laughed. "Aye. No frightening yon villagers."

They chatted amicably as they saddled their horses and added bags of cheese, bread, and dried jerky to break their fast. There was a small inn to eat a noon meal, though if resentment toward the English was still high in the village, Simon and his men would be ravenous by nightfall.

Simon accepted his sword from the armorer then slid it into the sheath at his belt. He checked the placement of daggers and added a mace to a strap on his saddle, while his soldiers attended their weapons. The moon had settled behind the trees and the sky lightened toward dawn when they rode into the village of Friar's Hill.

⫸⫷

ISEABAL GLANCED UP at the sound of hoof beats coming down the road behind them. Her heart skipped a beat. She whirled. "Quick! Aggie, Hew, get Ewan off the road!"

The village was only a short distance away, but there was no time to try to reach safety. In the pre-dawn light, they were too visible on the road, and they'd never outrun the galloping horses. Aggie stepped inside a cluster of three saplings, dragging Ewan with her. She knelt, sweeping her cloak around them for added protection. Shep crouched next to Ewan, lips curled to expose long white fangs. Hew peered from the protection of scrub, his weathered, lined face almost perfectly hidden in the crisscross of shadows.

Iseabal took a stance behind the broad trunk of a tree. Horses swept past. Iseabal held her breath, praying they would not be seen. Praying Ewan would remain silent, that Shep would not bark a challenge. Had James's men tracked them here?

Her fingers brushed against the slender, braided wool sling hanging at her belt. It gave her courage, for her elder brother—may he rest in peace—had thought it adequate as a lass' weapon and insisted she spend hours practicing. It still amused her to keep her skills sharp, and she'd brought it to hunt rabbits along their journey.

She drew the braided cord from her belt and slipped her finger through the loop at one end. Kneeling, she felt about for a handful of small stones and slipped one inside the cradle at the midpoint then palmed the thick knot at the other end.

The drum of hooves rumbled to a halt too close for comfort.

Dogs barked. Shouts of surprise rose. Sheep bleated. The din pounded her ears.

English raiders in Friar's Hill? Iseabal gripped the sling letting it sway gently, ready to loose the stone at a moment's notice.

Shouts from the other side of the village captured her attention. Grim satisfaction twisted her lips. *The English will regret their decision to raid this night.*

The noise increased. Steel clanged. A woman screamed. Visions of the battle at Eaglesmuir rose in her memory and she closed her eyes, attempting to blot out the sight that hovered in her mind. Hoof beats drew near. Angry shouts. The whistle of steel and the sloppy sound of a sword cutting deep into flesh. Shouts of victory and cries of pain pierced the night.

Iseabal's eyes flew open. Wide-eyed, she edged to her left enough to peer about the tree trunk. Pale sunlight glinted off unsheathed swords and axes. Horses' harnesses jingled. Bodies littered the ground.

The battle was over in a matter of minutes. A few riders pelted up the road, their shaggy ponies' ears flattened, nostrils flared wide. Two men were pulled roughly to their feet, hands bound by men wearing bright metal helmets.

They arenae Scots. Iseabal's heart stuttered. *Those were Scottish ponies fleeing north. Do the English hold Friar Hill?*

Their plan for sheltering safely with Aggie's family evaporated as Iseabal realized they now stood on English soil. Her anticipation of finding sanctuary lurched into fear for their lives.

>>>><<<<

SIMON WIPED HIS bloody blade on the cloak of a dead Scot. He had no idea who would claim responsibility for this raid, but he'd find out soon enough.

"Search the area! Bring any survivors to me."

"My lord! A woman in the trees!"

A dog barked, challenging the soldier. The man drew his sword and stalked toward the trees. The woman stepped from her shelter, blading her body sideways, something in her hand. Simon shouted a warning. She swung her arm in an arc, something long and slender fluttering from her hand. The soldier collapsed to the ground with a grunt.

Simon's chin jerked in surprise.

"What the . . .?"

He stared at the downed man then back at the woman. She was gone.

"Find her!" he shouted. Three soldiers rushed past, lining the road, peering into the woods with care.

A dog darted from the dense scrub and launched himself at one of the men. The soldier flung his arm up with a cry. The flash of black and white fur disappeared into the woods. Blood dripped from the soldier's forearm.

This was to have been a simple visit with the villagers. Simon's men carried weapons, but had not worn full armor. Simon swore. He would not make this mistake again.

The area was in an uproar. Men dashed into the woods, stealth abandoned. Another soldier cried out.

"Damn!" Simon glanced at his men fanned out behind him. A Scot stood defiantly between two soldiers, upper arms grasped firmly in leathered hands. Another sat sprawl-legged on the ground. Garin pointed to the road.

"They have her."

Simon stared. His men may have captured the woman, but she'd not made it easy. One soldier limped down the road, another held a palm to his forehead. Two soldiers gripped the woman's arms, one to either side. Even secured she shrugged first one shoulder then the other, as if they'd release her.

Behind her straggled an old woman, a wizened old man, and a lad of young years.

Scruffy group of Scots. It wasn't worth punishing them for defiance. He doubted his men wished to report they'd almost been bested by this ragged group. He'd give them a stern warning and send them on their way.

Simon stepped closer. A soldier shoved the woman's hood away and Simon found himself staring into the greenest eyes he'd ever . . . he shook his astonishment away.

"Bring her to the keep."

CHAPTER SIX

I SEABAL FROZE. FEAR and anger had blinded her, but the sight of the blond Englishman stopped her as effectively as a slap in the face.

It couldnae be. It isnae.

The sun was barely up and she was exhausted. That was the explanation. For whatever reason, the man before her looked very much like the man she'd rescued from a battlefield five years earlier. An English knight she'd never thought to see again. Yet, here he stood.

She must keep her wits about her.

She squared her shoulders and gave a subtle shake of her head when Aggie brought her attention to Ewan, needing Aggie to keep the lad at her side. The lad's features were all Maxwell, but his angelic blond hair was an exact replica of the man before her.

Ewan began to cry. Iseabal glanced about, looking for Shep.

"Where is the lad's dog?" she demanded.

The soldiers exchanged glances. "He's in the trees yon. He should come 'round soon."

Iseabal bristled. "Ye injured a lad's dog?"

A man held up his bleeding arm. "He bit me."

"He was protecting the lad!" Iseabal fired back.

Simon de Bretteby raised a hand. "Find the dog."

He gave Iseabal a long look and she regretted bringing Ewan to his attention. The boy and dog had formed a close bond, and Ewan had relied on Shep during the past tumultuous weeks. Shep often calmed Ewan when neither Iseabal nor Aggie could, and when Iseabal must be away from him, shielding him from the anger and fear at Eaglesmuir as her da lay dying, then as James had taken over the keep. To lose Shep was unthinkable.

Aggie folded Ewan against her skirts and Hew shuffled from one foot to another.

Simon glanced over his shoulder. "Get the injured and prisoners back to the keep."

A half dozen or so English soldiers loaded the horses and rode away, leaving an armed escort behind. A moment later, a man strode from the woods, Shep draped over his shoulders. The dog stirred at Ewan's shout. The soldier placed the dog on the ground where he stood, feet spread a bit, tail wagging gently as Ewan threw his arms about his neck and buried his face in the soft fur.

"Ye will come with me."

Simon's command doused Iseabal's relief at seeing Shep returned to Ewan. She tilted her head forward, allowing straggling hair to fall about her face, hoping Simon hadn't recognized her, knowing from the look he'd given her and the tone of his words his curiosity was at least piqued.

There was no future for us five years ago, though I was foolish enough to think I'd follow him anywhere. Nothing good can come of this now.

She could have struggled again, could have made it not worth their trouble to set her upon a horse. Refused to be taken to the keep, for Simon had no reason to detain her. But her defiance impacted Ewan, Hew, and Aggie, and she would barter for their freedom first.

MEMORIES ASSAILED SIMON on the ride back to North Hall.

Was this why he'd dreamed of Iseabal lately? She clearly had followed the natural course for a woman, taking her from the bloom of womanhood to motherhood. Though the light was yet low, it kissed her pale skin, enhanced the glow of her eyes. She was changed, certainly, her figure—what he could determine from the drape of her cloak—now ripe in the places once slender and young. He'd no expectation she would be the same girl he'd known five years earlier. It was clear she was married, perhaps loved. The child was enough to prove he had no right to her after he'd abandoned her . . . .

Damn. He hadn't wanted to leave her. But what else could he have done? He'd been a knight sworn to the de Wylde brothers, his duty to The Saint suspended as he retreated to the monastery to heal. Bringing a Scottish lass to an English keep hadn't seemed his best option.

He glanced at the mounted men next to him, captives carefully distributed among them. It was all he could do to keep from insisting she ride with him instead of his captain. That was one folly he managed to avoid. But seeing her seated before Garin tweaked his ire.

The sun was bright as they dismounted and led their prisoners into the hall. The two Scottish reivers were shoved into a corner where a soldier examined their wounds. Simon's eyes followed the woman and the small group at her heels. After noticing the calming effect the dog had on the boy, he decided not to order the beast from the room. A crying child was all he needed to push his morning beyond endurance. An unexpected attack by raiding Scots, one man dead, another wounded. Not at all how he'd envisioned his search for provisions and workers.

Garin stood close, his words for Simon's ears only. "I left two men tracking a blood trail through the woods. I will let ye know when the villain is found."

"I care not if he is brought back dead or alive."

Garin gave a curt nod and retreated from the room.

Simon sat in the lord's chair and surveyed his captives.

"Come forward."

Light flickered from torches on the wall and sunlight fell through arrow slits in the thick walls. Candles added their glow to the open room. There was little chance he could miss the defiant tilt of Iseabal's chin at his command. A soldier lifted a hand to her shoulder when she failed to obey, but Simon shook his head and the man's hand fell away.

"I wish to speak with ye, Iseabal. Please step forward where we needn't shout at one another."

Still she hesitated, though she did not deny her name. Smoothing her hair from her face, she moved forward to stand before him.

He smothered a grin. She'd been hiding from him. Which meant she knew full well who he was. Was her visit planned? Did she have anything in common with the raiders? It was ridiculous to think she'd risk an old man and woman, and *her son* . . . .

His mood changed abruptly. She was a Scot. Everything she did was suspect.

"What are ye doing here?"

She arched a fine brow. "At yer invitation, m'lord."

He frowned. "Damnit, Iseabal, I don't mean at the keep. What are ye doing so far from home? Why are ye on the road at night?"

She shrugged. "'Tis nae so far. Aggie has kin in Friar's Hill."

He nodded at the old woman. "Her kin? What of yours?"

ISEABAL GLANCED ABOUT the room. Men, still bristling with weapons, sat and stood about. Two men awaited their fate in the corner of the room, though she was heartened to see one had been accorded a bandage about his head. Simon clearly had a bit of humanity about him. Or mayhap he wished to save the men for a different fate.

One of the bound men grinned at her and she took a step back in shock. Was she so exhausted she imagined he was one of James's men? He would not have traveled this far. Would he?

Simon cleared his throat and Iseabal jerked her attention to answering his question.

"As I said, Aggie has kin in the village. We wished to visit."

"Nothing more?"

"Ye cannae hold me here. We have done nothing wrong." Her voice sharpened. Ewan wailed and broke from Aggie's grip. Ignoring Shep, he plunged into Iseabal's arms. She lifted him and he clung tightly to her, his body shaking.

"He has seen things this night a child shouldnae see. Let us go."

Aggie stepped hesitantly to her side, clearly upset

by the battle they'd found themselves in the midst of, only a shadow of her normal assured self.

"There is naught more we can tell ye. I must see to my son, my friends. Ye may be a hardened warrior, but they are gentle folk. And a wee lad who has endured too much."

Simon's intent gaze lingered on her, then swept to Ewan. "Escort them to the village. See to it they are reunited with their kin."

Relief sagged Iseabal's body. She accepted the soldier's company, admitting she'd been shaken by the deadly raid.

Aggie led them to the edge of the village to a small croft where sheep clustered in small pens next to a low shed. New lambs bleated and tottered on wobbly legs beneath the bellies of their recently sheared dams. The tang of animal urine mingled with scent of fresh grass and the earthy aroma of dung. A wagon, partially filled with refuse, a two-pronged wooden fork leaning against it, stood to one side.

A stout woman appeared in the doorway of the low building, wiping her hands and forearms with a strip of old linen, her skirts tucked up in her belt to keep them out of the churned mud of the pen. A single lamb tottered at her heels.

"Mary!" Aggie cried. The woman gave a startled shout then rushed through the milling sheep. She maneuvered through the gate and managed to latch it without so much as a lamb slipping past and flung her arms about Aggie.

"'Tis good to see ye, Sister," she said, pulling back with a grin. "And who have we here?" Her grin disappeared. "Consortin' with the English, are ye?"

"Lads from the keep," Aggie answered with a dismissive wave. "We ran into a bit of trouble this morning—in the middle of a raid, we were—and the lord himself sent these braw lads to be certain we arrived safely."

Mary harrumphed. "They are in good hands," she said, her voice rising. "I will see to it they come to no harm."

The soldiers paused, but wheeled their horses about at Iseabal's nod. She stepped forward.

"I am Iseabal Maxwell. Aggie has been Ewan's nurse since he was born, and my friend before that. She has spoken of ye fondly over the years."

Mary grinned. "Which is to mean she has offered ye a place to stay here with me and mine. Och, an extra hand is always welcome, especially at lambing, and we've enough food to fill yer bellies as well. Clyde has gone with the dogs for ewes who dinnae come down from the hills last week." She hooked a thumb over her shoulder. "Wil-me-lad is cleaning the pens."

"I'm grateful to ye, Mary. We willnae be a bother, and are pleased to do whatever work is needed. Mayhap Shep will be of help as well. He is a good sheepdog." Iseabal's chest tightened. Aggie had been right to lead them here. Her sister had made them welcome, and tears threatened behind Iseabal's eyes to realize they once again had a home.

Ewan wiggled down and hurried to the low fence. He dropped to his knees and poked his hand through the rails. The lamb that had followed Mary from the small barn grabbed his fingers between his lips and suckled hard. Ewan laughed and squirmed.

Iseabal's heart swelled. It would be a wonderful home.

⋙⋘

SIMON PACED THE dim corridor to the cell where the prisoners were held. Damned Scots. Their raid had cost him a seriously wounded knight as well as the deaths of two villagers. Justice would be swift.

Garin approached. "The trail led nowhere. I have sent others to scour the area, but it appears the wounded Scot has escaped."

Simon sent him an angry look, knowing it wasn't Garin's fault, but still smoldering from the encounter with the damned reivers.

A guard produced a massive metal key and opened the door. Striped with shadows and light from the barred window far above, the two Scots sat motionless, chained to the wall. Fresh blood stained the bandage on one man's head. The other glanced up as the door opened.

"I will know your names," Simon stated.

The slim, wiry man spit into the rushes on the floor. "'Tis nane of yer business," he said, the words slurred, his jaw swollen on one side.

"Ye will share it with the hangman, then."

The man scowled and his shoulders drooped. "Thom. Of Clan Maxwell."

Simon paused. Garin had been right. The Maxwells had indeed chosen to ride to Friar's Hill. Yet there had been no forewarning.

"Which Maxwell? Your men were poorly armed

and appeared to lack the finesse of most reivers."

Thom shrugged. "We'd mayhap had a bit too much to drink, though the ride sobered a few of us. We werenae expecting an armed resistance."

"Who is your leader?"

A sly grin crept over Thom's swollen face. "The lord and master of the wee lassie ye had in yer hall."

"Ye know her?"

"She's a wanted woman."

"Wanted? Explain."

The man shrugged. "She's a runaway. Pledged to my lord to be his wife. We tracked her, but dinnae expect she'd get so far, what with a bairn and all."

"Ye were following her?"

The man's eyes lit mockingly. "Nae. We were after sheep."

"Ye know the penalty for raiding." It wasn't a question.

"Hanging."

"Tell me what else ye know of her."

"Will ye return her to Maxwell? He has a fondness for the lass." The man grinned and made a rude gesture with his hand.

Simon gritted his teeth. "Not a chance."

CHAPTER SEVEN

I SEABAL GLANCED UP, Ewan's laughter better than all the potions, herbs, and draughts in a healer's bag for the grief in her heart. Even though life at Eaglesmuir had caused her much strain and worry, and her father had been a difficult man on his best days, the loss of family and home still ached deep in her heart.

She'd anticipated Ewan's questions and concerns, sleepless nights and night terrors, but in the past two days he had shown little of the horrors he'd seen and endured. This morning's sunshine seemed to gild her entire soul with golden light, and seeing Ewan playing happily with Shep and two orphan lambs lifted her spirits further.

From the corner of her eye, she caught sight of a man on a horse. Framed by the trees beyond the fields surrounding the croft, his outline blurred then was gone.

Was she imagining things? Could James know she

was here?

Impossible. It had only been two days since they'd arrived and she was uncomfortably aware the prisoners in Simon's keep now resided in graves beyond the kirkyard. At least he hadn't left them hanging from a post as a warning to other reivers. They'd been given no opportunity to alert James to her whereabouts. And she'd been hidden in the trees whilst Simon and his men routed the Maxwell bastards. None could have seen her.

A shudder rippled down her spine. Dead men could not carry tales. Would James attempt to avenge his lost men? She didn't know him well enough to predict if he would remain at Eaglesmuir with his tail tucked between his legs, or rally his men for another attack. She *did* know he was a bully, which meant he valued his own hide—likely above the perceived honor of seeking vengeance for the death of his men.

She shook her head. Only a fool would attack North Hall. It would take a dedicated force to overrun the keep, and she'd noted *radgie* brutes among James's men, not military geniuses able to successfully carry out a siege.

She peered into the woods, but the figure, shadow,

whatever had caught her attention, was gone. Picking a shirt from her basket of mending, she threaded her needle and set her mind to patching the hole in the elbow of one sleeve. Ewan's high-pitched giggles merged with the song of birds overhead and the bleating of lambs as they scampered about the pen.

'Twas a morning such as this. A bit of mist had clung to the trees, the sun not yet burning through the morning fog. Birdsong and the dense aroma of grass and soil after a rain.

She smoothed the rough fabric beneath her fingertips, remembering the coarse, stubbled feel of Simon's cheek and neck as she'd checked for signs of life. His skin, pale beneath smudges of dirt, a bruise blooming a purple shadow along one side of his head, had been cold to the touch, the warmth of life flickering faintly within. Lips blue-tinged from a night without shelter, parted with a whisper of sound breathing between them.

His eyelids had fluttered at her touch, then opened, revealing midnight eyes that stared at her, yet didn't.

It hadn't seemed right to turn the confused man over to her da, though it would have been a point of pride to capture an English knight. She'd hid him in a deserted croft, completely defying her da's orders.

And she'd fallen in love with her English knight. And lost him. Looking back, perhaps she'd been enamored with the idea of love. What did she know of love after only sixteen summers? Her son Ewan had taught her about love, not Simon.

She'd never thought she'd see Simon again, yet he ruled North Hall keep, not over a mile away.

Longing warred with resentment.

He claimed to be a knight bound to a lord, a third son with no destiny of his own. An Englishman. Unable to marry a Scottish lass.

Fear rose. Would he recognize his son?

Iseabal's gaze slid back to the present. A man on horseback broke from the tree cover and rode toward her. Iseabal sprang to her feet, but he merely gave her a slight nod as he passed, and rode to the croft where he dismounted and spoke to Mary.

I am jumping at shadows . . . . She frowned. He had been watching her. She was certain of it. Stuffing the shirt into her basket of mending, Iseabal walked to the croft, glancing at the man as she passed.

He was English, his voice unmistakable. Polite enough, though her first reaction was an affront to his presence. Perhaps this close to the Border, people based their likes and dislikes on how they were treated, not which king they supported.

The chill of suspicion lingered and she grabbed her cloak from the peg near the door. She set the basket on a bench and hurried to Ewan's side. He beckoned her near with excited hands.

"Look, Ma!" He tapped one of the lambs lightly between his ears then darted away. The knobby-kneed creature stared at Ewan then chased after him, his entire body bobbing up and down with youthful awkwardness. Ewan halted and the lamb, excited by the game, butted Ewan's belly. Ewan grunted and dropped to his butt with an *oof* of surprise. Before Iseabal could react, he grinned.

"His head is hard!"

Shep darted between the lamb and lad, using his body to separate the two.

"A moment too late, Sheppy," Iseabal scolded. "Ye must take better care of yer lad."

The rider mounted his horse and rode away. Iseabal's gaze followed until he was lost from view. She turned thoughtfully to Mary and crossed the yard to hold a ewe still while Mary led a bumbling newborn lamb to the proper end of its anxious ma.

"Do ye oft have Englishmen here?"

"Och, 'tis nae verra common. But he wished to know if mutton could be bought for the lord's table." She gave a satisfied nod as the lamb latched on to a teat and began to nurse vigorously. "I willnae have him takin' my ewes, and the lambs willnae be ready for a few months. But we've some older hoggets that dinnae go to market last year and will make a nice contribution to the table."

Mary motioned for Iseabal to precede her from the pen, leaving the ewe and her new baby to themselves.

"'Tis all he wanted?" Iseabal felt foolish for asking, but she still couldn't shake the thought he'd been staring at her for some time before he rode up.

"He hinted the lord at the hall might send us business if we wanted it. 'Tis a five-day wonder, to be sure. After all the uproar with the Johnstone's lambs the other night, 'tis a pleasant chance to be exchanging beasts for coin. Auld man Johnstone's wife Milly is still a'bed after being knocked down by one of those ruffians. I will take them a basket of bread tomorrow and see how she fares."

"Has he, the man just now, has he been here before?"

Mary winked and nudged Iseabal with an elbow. "Taken a fancy to 'im, eh? Might be nice to have another Scottish lassie at the hall."

Iseabal stared, shocked. "What? No! I havenae taken a fancy to anyone. He ... reminded me of someone."

"Weel, ye and the laddie need a home of yer own someday—not that I'm runnin' ye off, mind ye. I'm pleased for the help and the company, and thankful ye brought my sister home. But a bonnie lass as yerself needs a husband around, and the lad needs a da to look up to, teach him how to be a man."

Iseabal gathered her scattered wits and managed a smile.

"Thank ye, Mary. I will think on it."

Iseabal pivoted slowly on her heel. *I prefer a nice Scottish lad, thank ye verra kindly.* Iseabal sniffed and took two steps, then halted, her thoughts pulled to James and his ilk.

Mayhap I should remain unmarried. I dinnae like broken hearts, unkept promises, or brutish behavior. 'Tis all I have seen from the men in my life, and I willnae go back.

Ewan dashed across the yard and tugged at her skirt. "I'm hungry, Ma."

She knelt and brushed a dirt smudge from his cheek. "We will find ye a bite, then, my wee *chield*. Come with me."

><<

SIMON STARED THROUGH the trees at the black-haired woman as she knelt beside the boy. Taking his hand, she rose and they strolled toward the croft, the shaggy dog at their heels. A fist of regret twisted in his gut.

I could change nothing. Our worlds are too different. Yet I cannot abide the thought of her in another man's arms, bearing his child. A son.

Garin reined his horse to a halt next to him. "The woman suspects she is being watched. She gave me curious glances as I rode up. *Not* the nice kind. And I'm used to *very* nice looks from ladies."

Simon ignored Garin's gibe. "She must be protected. Word will get back to James Maxwell that his two henchmen's necks are several inches longer than the last time he saw them, and resting beneath good English soil. Maxwell, being unpredictable and unprincipled, may make the mistake of making an attempt at retribution."

"Ye just sent him scurrying back to his keep with a beating he won't soon forget. Do ye truly believe he is foolish enough to risk a second beating?"

"I don't know the man well enough to say. Our riders have visited various inns to gather whatever information and gossip they can, to no avail. There is still one man unaccounted for who witnessed the exchange with Iseabal and us immediately after the battle. If she is indeed Maxwell's intended, could word have gotten back to him of her presence here? I do not like an enemy I do not know or understand."

He ran a hand over the back of his neck to relieve tension at the base of his skull. "Should he return for Iseabal, he will attempt to take her. I will not allow it."

"We could spread the word she is in the village. If we drew him here, we could put swift end to his scheming."

Simon sliced his hand through the air. "No. She has seen and endured enough. I will not use her as bait. Not if my life depended on it."

"Then we will protect her," Garin replied with a shrug. "Howbeit, if ye brought her to the hall, it would make our job easier."

Simon shot him a startled look. "She would not agree. It would be unseemly. She is unwed . . . ."

"She flees an unwanted marriage. A good reason for her to seek refuge at the keep."

Simon frowned. He could make quite a list of possibilities of why Iseabal should shelter at North Hall rather than a shepherd's croft outside the village. All of which involved him. Unreasonably, the fact irritated him. He shouldn't want the Scotswoman. But he did.

"We will have a man watch her discreetly. Until I can determine she is not in danger, she will have at least some protection."

Garin nodded. "As ye wish. 'Twill be no hardship to sit and watch a pretty woman a few hours every day."

Simon shot him a quelling look, eyes narrowed, lips tilted in a frown. "Ye will treat her with every respect and report to me anything at all suspicious."

"Of course," Garin replied, a raised eyebrow betraying the smile he struggled to hide. He gave a short nod and reined his horse away. His muted voice drifted over his shoulder.

"Kaily will not like this."

Kaily does not have a say in what I do to protect

people on my land. The thought surprised Simon. He neither needed nor wanted a woman's council, least of all his leman's. Would he listen to *Iseabal's* council? Five years ago, she'd been charming, uncomplicated, easy to talk to. For nearly a sennight he'd enjoyed being cared for by a beautiful young woman, worries for his duty dulled by the lingering effects of the blow he'd taken to his head.

Once he'd left the croft, his life had returned to its normal activities, though he'd often thought of her over the following months. Her memory had eventually faded—almost. Just when he was in a position to take a wife, whether he was interested in marriage or not, Iseabal had entered his life.

Kaily was *not* going to like this.

CHAPTER EIGHT

TWO RANKS OF mounted knights and their squires, bowmen and other attendants, filed through the double gates of the keep, swelling the number of people in the hall to an alarming number, and threatening to stretch the skills of cook and her assistants. Simon couldn't have been happier.

"I understand why The Saint did not send this many men at the beginning, but 'tis good to see them now."

"We would have spent all our time trying to feed them," Garin agreed. "We now have the keep in good repair, thanks to the people of Friar's Hill, and can expand the everyday challenges of de Wylde's outpost."

"The villagers were not averse to our money," Simon noted. "But the workmanship is sound and likely to last many years."

The whinnies of horses and rumble of men's voices mixed with the clatter and clang of bits and swords and spurs. The leader of the knights dismounted and strode to Simon.

"My lord, I am Sir Charlys of Greenthorne. My lord, Baron de Wylde, has placed me in charge of these men, and we are yours to command."

Simon nodded gravely. "I am pleased to receive ye and your men at North Hall." He tilted his head to his new steward. "Alane will see the accommodations are handled."

Alane ducked his head and vanished into the melee in the yard.

Simon gestured into the hall. "A drink and mayhap a bite whilst they sort things out?"

Charlys grinned. "I knew I'd like it here."

They settled at the upper table and a serving girl filled mugs with ale then placed a platter of assorted sliced meats and cheeses before them. With a bobbed curtsy, she scurried off.

"Any word from the baron?" Simon took a sip then settled back in his chair.

"He approves of your having sent men to assess the danger James Maxwell could be. He's somewhat familiar with the father, Albert. Albert and *his* father, the clan chief, are from the same mold—harsh but reasonably fair—but word is the son is a brute."

Simon frowned. "Then we shall double our guard to the north. I will not have him attacking the villagers again. Friar's Hill may have a rough history between Scots and English, but we will give them as much protection as we can."

"Ye are passionate about yer duty," Charlys noted.

"As long as I am lord here, I will take the welfare of the people very seriously."

Charlys nodded. "Fair enough. Keep the peace rather than burn out the problems."

Simon led Charlys through the daily workings of the keep. He at last turned Garin to a detailed discussion of the duty roster and took his leave, ready to be shed of the more formal tunic he'd donned to welcome the newcomers.

He opened the door to his chamber and came to a full stop. His eyes widened and after a brief hesitation, he stormed into the room.

Kaily spun about, apprehension and an attempt at cheerfulness warring in her eyes. She held a gown before her like a shield, gaze darting to the enormous pile of similar garments piled on the bed.

"Do . . . do ye like it?" She held the blue fabric beneath her chin and swayed a bit to one side. "I will have a chest brought up to store these in. The bed will be cleared by nightfall."

"Ye will move the chest—and yer gowns—to another bedroom," Simon growled. The sheer profusion of feminine garments draped over the room and his armor stand staggered him. He stalked the chamber, filching filmy, lacy articles of clothing from atop his chain mail and helmet. With a fist full, he approached Kaily.

"I did not bring ye here to set up in my rooms. I did not give ye permission to add yer accoutrements to mine. This was a temporary arrangement, not . . . ." He gestured about the room he scarcely recognized. "Not a bid for a wife."

"Ye will not marry me?" Kaily shrieked. "I have sacrificed the past sennight, my reputation, *and* my virtue to a man who will not marry me?"

"Slightly longer than a sennight, and yer virtue was sacrificed to others long ago," Simon growled.

"Ye are hateful!" she sobbed. She flounced onto the edge of the bed, raking the hem of her gown up the length of one shapely leg. Cutting a calculating look over her shoulder, she resumed her sobs, shielding her face behind her palms.

Simon hesitated. Kaily's body was luscious—and he knew every inch of it. Was he truly sending her back to Berwyck Castle? Or simply reminding her of the boundaries of their relationship?

Kaily slid slowly off the bed. Her gown pooled in her lap, revealing her thighs, enticingly bare. Simon took a step forward. His breath deepened as his heartbeat kicked up a notch. He stared at all she offered then held out a hand. She placed her palm in his and he lifted her to her feet. Drawing her close, he kissed her cheek.

"I will not be manipulated," he breathed softly. "Pack your bags and prepare to return to Belwyck Castle."

Kaily hissed and snatched her hand away then took a step back. "Lady de Wylde will not be pleased. She is my friend."

She whirled in a rage of skirts. Snatching up her belongings, she flung them into the open chest. The room was cleared in a matter of moments, though Simon imagined the dresses would require some care once they were unpacked. Which mattered not a whit to him.

Kaily grabbed an embroidered cloak. She placed a hand on the door latch and flung a furious look over her shoulder.

"This is not over between us!" Yanking the door open, she stormed from the room.

"Oh, yes, sweet Kaily, it most certainly is."

"SAINT CUTHBERT'S WEE prick!"

Iseabal came to a halt on Mary's heels and peered around her into the gloom of the sheep fold. Sunlight slanted across the floor from an opening where wooden slats lay broken on the ground. Ewes milled about, drifting close to the gap, their loyalty to the flock keeping them from escaping.

"Help me count the wee blighters," Mary said with a harrumph of frustration, indicating the ewes with a sweep of her hand.

Iseabal immediately began counting. She lost track in the sea of white bodies and started over. "I count thirty-eight."

Mary bit back a curse. "We've a pair o' lasses missing. The ewes in this pen havenae lambed yet, so they dinnae have a bairn at their sides." She rubbed the back of her neck. "I'll look for the ornery besoms after I get this batch fed."

"I'll do it. It looks as if 'twill rain soon, and I can hope to be back before the weather is too bad."

"Och, ye dinnae know yer way about, nor where the sheep are likely to head. Dinnae fash yerself, lass. I'll see to it."

"Dinnae be ridiculous. I can spend my time tramping the moors and the ewes need to be found before . . . ." Iseabal stopped, not wanting to imagine the ewes hunted by wolves. If they lambed in the open, the wobbly newborns could easily fall prey to a number of animals. "Ye are needed here. Aggie can watch Ewan, and I will take Shep with me."

Mary shrugged. "Take a bit o' food with ye and some bandaging cloths. Ye never know what mischief they've gotten into."

Iseabal nodded, firming her decision to leave Ewan with his nurse. He might find tramping about in the rain fun for a bit, but finding a wounded—or dead—ewe or lamb would break his young heart. After telling Aggie where she was going, she kissed Ewan's protests away, promising to bake a cake when she returned.

She collected a basket of the items Mary suggested

and draped her wool cloak over her head. She threaded her sling through her belt and hefted a stout walking stick for added protection. Whistling Shep to her side, she set off through the thickening mists.

THE GRAY SPRING morning quickly turned blustery. The wind lashed the misty rain. Iseabal headed up the slopes of the moors where the sheep were released to graze after lambing. She slipped once, her boot sucked into a boggy patch. Iseabal clutched her cloak tighter and followed Shep's bounding gait around bits of scrub and rock.

She'd fallen quite a bit behind when she heard Shep's bark.

"A moment, laddie! I'm coming!"

Quickening her pace, she climbed over stones and skirted marshy areas, at last reaching the dog. He stood guard over two ewes and a wee lamb that trembled violently in the cold wind.

"Och, ye poor thing!" Iseabal squatted beside the lamb and grabbed a cloth from her basket. She rubbed the wool briskly, drying the birth fluid from his coat.

"Which one of ye is his ma?" she questioned, her teeth chattering as a gust of rain-laden air blew her hood from her head. One of the ewes bleated and, lifting her tail, deposited another lamb at Iseabal's feet. The ewe swiveled about, peering at the new lamb as though startled to see it. She nosed it roughly, pushing it to its feet. The other ewe chuckled deep in her throat in an encouraging manner.

"Do *not* have another," Iseabal scolded, fully aware triplets were not at all uncommon, "if ye expect me to carry yer brood home. Two is all I can manage."

She set aside the first lamb and pulled another cloth from her basket. She dried the second lamb as much as she could, then wrapped them each against the cold. Sitting back on her heels to survey her handiwork, she heard Shep's warning growl a moment before he exploded into furious barking.

Pivoting about, she swept hair and rain from her face, peering into the gray gloom.

Two shadows darker than the gray rain and mist shifted, one to either side. Golden eyes sparkled in the gloom. Quivering lips swept back, showing glistening white teeth.

Wolves!

Iseabal reached for the sling at her belt, crouching lower, her opposite hand sweeping the ground for stones to fit the cradle. She cursed as one of the ewes bleated, drawing the wolves nearer. Setting a rock in the web of the sling, she leapt to her feet, swinging the sling in an arc just behind her right shoulder as her brother had taught her. The two wolves hunkered down at her threat and growled a warning.

Seizing the opportunity, Iseabal released the sling, stepping into the throw to give it more power. The rock whipped through the air, striking one wolf in the head. He yelped and drew back. Shep leapt at the wolf and was lost in a flurry of snarling fur. Iseabal, her sling already reloaded, launched a rock at the second wolf. He slunk backward, but the stone struck his body.

The sheep bleated in fear and the second wolf circled to the side. Iseabal slung another rock, striking him again, but he would not be deterred. Angry and terrified, Iseabal stomped her foot.

"Get by, ye beast! These arenae yer sheep!" She crouched to the ground seeking another handful of stones. The wolf leapt, clipping her shoulder and sending her stumbling backward. The wolf yelped then fell to the ground and was silent.

The first wolf faded away into the rain.

Iseabal stared dumbfounded at the dead wolf next

to her then scrambled to her feet.

"Shep?"

The dog whined and rose slowly to his feet, one paw dangling above the ground, the white of his ruff stained dark. Iseabal dropped to her knees beside him and hugged him close, tears blinding her eyes. He licked her face then stiffened, a low growl rattling his chest.

Iseabal spun about, a stone in her hand.

Dark lines like saplings sprouted where no trees had been minutes earlier. Rain pelted from black clouds covering the sun, dripping over the broad, wool-covered shoulders of a man on horseback no more than a few paces away.

Iseabal's throat dried. Her heart beat painfully in her chest. An ewe bleated plaintively behind her. Shep sidled against Iseabal, baring his teeth to the stranger.

CHAPTER NINE

SIMON BALANCED A dagger lightly between his fingers, ready to send it to join the other already buried in the wolf's body. His horse snorted and pawed the earth, a signal of unease as well as an intent to paw the predator into the ground. Two knights nudged their horses forward, one to either side.

Iseabal rose, blocking his aim. Her dog stood at her side, blood staining the white of the coat about his neck. Simon glanced past Iseabal and reassured himself the wolf on the ground did not move, then swung down from his horse. Garin took the reins. Steel *shushed* into scabbards as Garin and Richard sheathed their weapons.

"Are ye injured?" Simon's gaze swept her sodden form. Her black hair hung limp on either side of her face, pulling free from the twist of braids wrapped around her head. Raindrops clung to her dark lashes, green eyes sparkling. Mud coated the hem of her cloak.

A length of woven cloth hung from one hand and he understood the wolves' earlier startled reaction.

"Ye are skilled with a sling."

Iseabal glanced down at the empty weapon in her hand then drew the strings through the belt at her waist. "'Twasn't enough. I have ye to thank for dispatching yon beast." She rubbed her shoulder. "Had I not crouched for another rock, he would have struck me full on."

Her face, normally pale, whitened further. She wobbled then straightened her shoulders.

"I must tend to Shep, then return to the croft quickly. The lambs need shelter." She knelt at the dog's side and pushed aside the reddened fur, fingers probing through the wet coat.

"Let me help," Simon said, stepping forward.

"I can do it," she snapped.

Startled, Simon halted. "I know ye are capable. But 'tis getting darker and I do not know if the other wolf will return or not."

Iseabal paused. "Thank ye."

Simon squatted beside her and examined the dog's wound. "It still bleeds, yet does not appear life-threatening. His leg, howbeit, may require attention."

"We will travel slowly. I will carry the lambs." Iseabal reached for the drenched twins.

"Damned, but ye will not! North Hall is just atop the ridge. I will take ye there until this weather eases. All of ye need shelter, and your dog needs care."

"I cannae. I must go home." Iseabal's startling green eyes glowed beneath dark lashes.

"Ye helped *me* once," Simon murmured, laying a restraining hand on her shoulder. "This will require little effort and I risk nothing, yet it is a small measure of repayment for a past kindness."

She snorted and stood, drawing away. "Repayment? Risk? Ye have no idea."

"I have gained a bit of wisdom these past five years. I understand what could have happened should ye have been caught sheltering an English knight."

Iseabal shrugged. "I was young and foolish. I daresay I wouldnae risk such again."

Simon frowned. "Were ye punished?" The idea infuriated him, yet it would have been well within her father's right had she been caught in such disobedience.

Iseabal tilted her head. "Nae." She shuddered and glanced away.

Simon's frown deepened. Iseabal was cold, wet, and there was something between them that needed to be said. Damned if he was going to do it in the pouring rain.

"Get on the horse, Iseabal. I will hand the lambs up to ye."

She hesitated. Simon plowed past her and grabbed the lambs, ignoring the bleats of alarm and Shep's warning bark. "I'll not have your death on my hands. Get on the horse."

A warning slant of her chin reminded Simon his Scottish lass might not be the pliable young woman he remembered. He tempered the command.

"Please."

There was no fluttery coquettish grin of triumph, merely a slight softening of her posture before she acceded to his request and strode to the horse. She shoved her raised foot at the stirrup, but her aim was poor and she missed. Simon thrust the lambs at Richard then placed his hands at Iseabal's waist. Her body beneath the cloak was cold, stiff—and only partly because he laid hands on her, if his guess was accurate. Giving her a push, he set her in the saddle. He mounted behind her then nudged his horse into a slow walk, mindful of the injured dog and the sheep he wouldn't leave behind.

They wound their way up the slope, picking their way over and around rocks and boulders. The dog limped behind the sheep which clustered behind Richard's horse, following the bleating lambs.

The gate to the keep swung open at Simon's signal. They dismounted next to the door to the hall and two stable boys dashed through the rain to collect the horses. Iseabal insisted Richard give her the lambs, but at Simon's frown, the young knight carried the twins inside the hall, leaving word for someone to rouse the shepherd. Shep hobbled at Iseabal's heels, head down, tail drooping. Simon noticed silver grizzling the dog's muzzle and issued an instruction for blankets to be brought to the hearth for dog and beasts.

Half-afraid Iseabal would disappear if he left her side, Simon shed his drenched cloak next to the fire and handed his leather hauberk to a squire for cleaning. He stepped to the hearth and pulled Iseabal's cloak from her shoulders and spread it across a bench to dry.

She knelt beside the lambs and used one of the blankets to rub them briskly. Shep nosed the pair, licking their coats. Steam rose from Iseabal, the lambs, and the dog as the fire warmed them.

"Your skin is like ice," Simon noted, placing the backs of his fingers against Iseabal's cheek. She flinched as though he'd struck her, then redoubled her efforts to dry the lamb. The creature bleated.

"I have servants to help. Do not rub their coats away." Simon beckoned two women to the hearth. With an exchange of glances, Iseabal relinquished the lambs to their care. A third woman laid a tray of bandages and unguents on the bench beside the hearth and stroked the dog's head.

"Poor boy," she crooned. "What a good dog ye are to protect the lambs."

Iseabal actually smiled. Relief lanced through Simon. He took Iseabal's hand and raised her to her feet. "We must warm ye. Your charges are being cared for."

"Dinnae fash over me. I will dry quick enough by the fire."

"And have a lung inflammation on the morrow," Simon growled. "I can take better care of ye than that."

Glancing about the room, he spied Kaily as she crossed the hall, noting she and Iseabal were of a size. He called to her and waved her over.

"See if ye can spare a gown for our guest. Then bring her back to the hall."

Kaily's eyes widened, but she altered her course and led Iseabal from the room. Simon took the opportunity to grab the dry tunic Garin held out to him. Shedding his wet shirt left his skin prickling with cold, until the dry one settled warmly over his shoulders.

Garin bumped his arm then nodded to the doorway where Iseabal and Kaily had exited.

"I wouldn't say that was the smartest thing ye ever did."

Simon followed his gaze. "What?"

"Sending the woman ye're interested in off with yer mistress."

"Kaily isn't my mistress."

Garin's eyebrows rose. "Ye haven't proposed to the wench, have ye?"

Simon shook his head. "No. She's leaving the keep today."

Garin grunted. "Ye may be popular with the ladies, but ye do not understand them. Kaily will not be kind."

ISEABAL FOLLOWED THE Englishwoman in silence. The

rigid set of her shoulders spoke clearly of her dislike, though of what exactly, Iseabal did not know. Scottish hospitality would have been much warmer.

Iseabal shivered and rubbed her arms. The passageway was dark and cold as it wound to the rear of the keep. Torches flickered on the wall, generating smoke but little warmth.

The woman paused at a closed door, then knocked preemptively. The door opened and a young woman peered out. Her eyes widened and she bobbed her head.

"Aye, m'lady?"

"She needs something dry to wear."

Iseabal had no liking for the woman's high-handed manner, but the younger lass hastened to do her bidding.

Simon's chatelaine? His wife? A moment of commiserative pity washed over her. *He'll have his hands full with that one.*

A moment later, Iseabal was garbed in a plain brown dress, a slightly frayed surcoat over the top for added warmth. The gown's hem swung a few inches above her boots, but the relief of dry clothing pushed any dismay over improper fit from her mind.

"Thank ye," she said, glancing from the maid to the aloof woman who glared at her unkindly. "I ken what a sacrifice yer maid has made, offering me what is likely her second best gown. The generosity of her gift is much appreciated."

Her barb struck home. The older woman's skin flushed an unbecoming shade of purple. Iseabal shifted her attention back to the maid.

"My name is Iseabal. I will return yer gown to ye before I leave."

"Rosaline, m'lady," the maid ventured with a short bob of respect. "I thank ye."

Rosaline motioned for Iseabal to turn around, then quickly combed out Iseabal's hair and braided it, tucking an impudent wisp behind her ear. She then tugged and smoothed the gown and surcoat into place.

Iseabal's escort tapped her toe impatiently. She leaned close to Iseabal's ear. "Don't bother setting your cap for Sir Simon. He is deceitful," she hissed. Her nose in the air, she whirled and stalked from the room.

"Her name's Kaily," the maid whispered. "M'lord sent her packin' this morn."

His mistress. Ex-*mistress.*

Giving the maid a slight nod of understanding,

Iseabal followed Kaily. Her unhurried manner caught Kaily's impatient wave from the door.

"He will use ye and toss ye like so much spoiled meat," Kaily huffed. "Do not think to beguile a pledge from him. He isn't the marrying kind."

Iseabal hated to agree with her, but she'd already had her heart broken by the man, and could have given Kaily the exact same warning. Iseabal didn't want Simon and could have reassured Kaily of her lack of interest. Unfortunately, it appeared the woman was all but out the door, though it was difficult to imagine Simon's decision to be rid of his mistress had anything to do with her.

Iseabal gave a one-shouldered shrug. "Marrying an Englishman isnae something I wish, though I take yer warning as 'tis meant. One woman to another."

Kaily halted abruptly, casting a glance up and down the passageway as if to be certain they were not overheard.

"He was pleased enough to take me to his bed, and now refuses to accept responsibility and marry me." She tossed her head. "I am a *lady*, not one of his strumpets."

Iseabal wisely kept her rejoinder to herself. She'd

lain with the man as well, and had a child to show for it. Not that he'd ever get that information from her.

Her heart skipped a beat. Ewan would give Simon a son without the need to marry. She could not allow that to happen. Would he suspect Ewan was his son? Iseabal tried unsuccessfully to push aside her rising panic. She and Ewan had no place else to go. Friar's Hill was now their home, but with Simon lord of the village, Ewan would be too much in his sight. Simon was not a stupid man. It wouldn't take much for him to consider the lad's age and begin to ask questions.

Ewan's green eyes and broad forehead—his Max-well legacy—rose in her mind. She relaxed slightly. He looked nothing like Simon. Except for the golden curls gracing his head. They were exactly like Simon's.

CHAPTER TEN

KAILY HALTED ABRUPTLY, skirts swaying, eyes flashing, as Simon met them in the hall. His gaze glanced over her to Iseabal, noting her guarded look.

Damn! What did Kaily say?

Quelling the impulse to kick himself for sending her with Kaily, and ignoring Garin's *I-told-ye-so* look, he motioned for Iseabal to precede him and guided her back to her seat at the hearth. The dog thumped his tail on the floor as they approached, seemingly much improved with the healer's care and a dish of meaty broth brought up from the kitchen.

Iseabal ruffled the dog's ears, peering at his wounds. A bright white bandage wrapped about the dog's foreleg and the blood had been cleaned from his ruff. Apparently satisfied with the dog's treatment, Iseabal took the offered seat and a servant handed her a steaming cup of cider. The rich scent of apples rose and Iseabal's lips curved in appreciation as she wrapped her hands about the mug.

Simon frowned, then caught himself, and forced his lips into a gentler slope. "I am sorry ye were attacked. Ye must have known there are wolves about."

Iseabal rolled one shoulder as if she'd weighed the dangers and found them acceptable. Simon resisted the impulse to shake her. What if he hadn't arrived when he had?

"How did ye find me?" Her eyebrows lifted in question.

Simon bit the inside of his lip to stall his reply. Shrug it off as chance? Or tell her the truth?

Her eyes narrowed. "Ye've been following me." She set her mug down with a thud. "I'd like to go now." She pushed up from the chair. Simon grabbed her wrist, restraining her. Her look of warning sent daggers into his gut. He removed his hand.

"Wait until the rain stops. I promised I would take ye and your animals home as soon as the weather clears," her reminded her, wishing again he knew what Kaily had said. His gaze cut to the doorway.

Kaily flashed him a smug look as she left the hall.

Simon ground his teeth. "Whatever Kaily has told ye, know she is upset with me. Might ye give me the benefit of the doubt?" He motioned a request for Iseabal to return to her seat. With a lift of her chin, she sat.

"Ye think I dinnae understand the wrath of a spurned mistress?" One black eyebrow arched, laden with hauteur.

Simon's skin heated. He leaned closer, his words for Iseabal only. "I never meant to hurt ye. Our time was neither sordid nor casual. My regret was neither of us was of an age or in a position to make any sort of promise."

She glanced about the room. "Nae so bad for a third son with no prospects."

"Five years ago my entire life was fighting. I belonged to Lord de Wolfe. I then pledged my sword to his nephew, Geoffrey de Wylde, and there isn't a Scotsman alive who would have given me his daughter in marriage."

Iseabal sent him an amused look. "Ye would have married me? That warms my heart."

"Damnit, Iseabal! What will it take for ye to accept my apology?"

She drew a deep breath and slowly let it out. "Och, now ye're a landed lord, I suppose ye could use yer funds to sponsor a convent—a refuge for the poor victims of unscrupulous men."

Simon huffed, then realized she meant to torment him. Her tone was low, drawling, not the swift biting fury Kaily used when vexed. Iseabal might not like him, but she'd apparently moved beyond their liaison long ago.

He blinked. He wasn't certain he liked being so easily dismissed. He sought a different topic. Something that might bring a smile to her lips. "Tell me of your son. Is he much like his father?"

Her hands gripped the arms of the chair. The delicate color in her cheeks vanished.

"I am sorry," Simon said. "I do not know why everything I say causes ye pain. 'Tis not my intent."

Iseabal relaxed. "Ye cannae know mention of Ewan's da upsets me. 'Tis nae a subject I am fond of."

"What happened?"

Iseabal took her time before she answered. "He left to fight with the English and never returned."

"Again, I am sorry. The enmity between our people has cost us much."

"Aye." She fingered the lip of the mug.

"Do ye plan to remarry?"

"A dear friend has suggested Ewan needs a da."

"And ye? What about ye, Iseabal? Do ye need a husband?"

Her stark gaze met his.

"Nae."

⟫⟫⟫⟪⟪⟪

HER SKIN SUDDENLY cried for his touch. To know he'd recently held his mistress—kissed her, loved her—tore her heart from her chest. Kaily might be angry over the loss of a title, but Iseabal would have demanded far more. She would have claimed nothing less than his heart.

She had no right to him. He'd never promised he would take her with him. Her ears had worked perfectly when he warned her he would leave, resume his life as a knight in service to de Wolfe. It was her heart that had refused to listen.

She had his son. Mayhap he would wish to know he'd sired a child. It was also possible he had many by-blows and one more would scarcely interest him. Ewan was all she had left of the sweet folly of her youth, and she would not sacrifice her son or her memories to assuage her guilt for not telling Simon he was Ewan's father.

ISEABAL GRIPPED THE wagon's wooden seat, her eyes trained on the low gray horizon, and tried not to stare at the man on the bay gelding next to her. The wheels bumped over the rocky ground, pitching her back and forth. The lambs and the two ewes bedded down comfortably in deep hay—a scarcity this time of year— Shep curled next to them. She'd found and saved the silly bleating beasts. Why was her heart so grim?

Her gown was still slightly damp even after several hours draped over a rod near the hearth, and the brisk air bit through the cloth. But her sense of loss bit deeper. She stole a glance at Simon, seated atop his dark red war horse, black mane and tail flowing in the breeze. Simon's golden curls, shorn close beneath his helmet, were mercifully out of tempting view. She'd once run her hands through the locks, marveling as they twisted about her fingers. Her skin remembered the sensation as though it was yesterday.

His dark eyes stared straight ahead as if intent on avoiding her gaze. Little beyond words had passed between them during the strained hours at North Hall, and though she'd skirted acceptance of his apology, he hadn't asked her forgiveness again. Despite her avowal their brief acquaintance held no influence over her, he still had the power to wound her.

The careful shield she'd built around herself since she'd discovered she was pregnant five years past had sustained a direct hit this day. To her dismay, she found nothing more than a hollow space within the perimeter of her walls. Intent on allowing neither words nor actions to affect her decision to raise Ewan without the subterfuge of a willing husband to cloud the circumstances of his birth, she'd allowed nothing inside. No one to further complicate her feelings of betrayal and loss.

"I've made arrangements for someone to keep an eye on ye and the croft."

Simon's words snared her attention and she realized they'd come to a stop a short distance from Mary's and Clyde's croft.

"There's nae need . . . ."

He held up a hand, interrupting her protest. He dismounted, stripping off his helmet. He hung it on his saddle then stepped to the wagon. "I will not have ye bothered. When I determine ye are no longer at risk, we will discuss this again."

Iseabal scowled. "We are capable of caring for ourselves. We dinnae need the English . . . ."

"Caring, yes. Protecting is a different matter. Ye will not sway me on this."

"Why does it matter so much? I'm of nae importance to ye."

A muscle twitched in Simon's jaw. His eyes bored into hers.

"Suit yerself." Iseabal hopped down from the wagon before he could assist her. She did not wish his help—and she did not believe she could endure the torment of his hands on her, however impersonal.

"'Tis no bother to me if ye wish to squander yer knights' time sitting about the village when they could be doing something important." Her bravado strained to ring true. The truth was, every time she saw one of his knights, rather than worry James or one of his men had found her, she would know Simon watched.

Simon unhooked the boards at the back of the wagon and lowered Shep to the ground while the driver unloaded the two ewes. Mary's dog rushed from the sheep fold, barking his challenge. His posture changed at Iseabal's command to halt, and he sat in the middle of the dirt road, head tilted to one side as though perplexed.

Mary appeared in the doorway. Ewan pushed past her, racing across the yard.

"Ma!" He yanked open the gate and pelted up the road.

Iseabal's sore heart eased and she bent to hug Ewan. Shep's bark drew the lad's attention and he tore away, using his hands to pull himself up enough to look into the wagon.

"Mary, Aggie! More lambs!" he shouted as he bounced up and down, unable to maintain his position at the rear of the wagon. Simon caught Ewan and hefted him effortlessly next to the lambs.

Iseabal's breath halted. Late afternoon sunlight pierced dispersing clouds, gilding the two heads bent to examine the new lambs. She clenched her fists, wadding the damp thin wool between her fingers. Ewan laughed and tilted his face to Simon, green eyes meeting midnight blue. Iseabal's heart quivered.

Mary crossed the yard and gave Iseabal a hug. "We worried about ye, lass. 'Tis good to see ye took no harm." She peered into the wagon at Ewan's insistence. "And brought a bonnie pair back with ye." Her gaze cut to Ewan and Simon, a curious slant to her head.

Iseabal snapped her fingers. "Come down, Ewan. We must get the lambs in the fold before dark."

Simon sent her a curious look. "We've time. Don't be so hard on the boy."

Hard on him? I've raised him, not ye. Loved him, taught him . . . . Iseabal's eyes flew wide, her hand raising to her mouth as though she'd said the words aloud.

Simon's head tilted farther. "I'll not harm the boy." He stood only a step or two away, his voice pitched low, but to Iseabal it seemed as though he shouted.

"The ewe. She'll be wanting her lambs." It was hardly an apology, but her urgent goal was to take Ewan away from Simon. Away from Mary's thoughtful gaze, before even an innocent comparison ruined everything.

With a slight nod, Simon set the lambs on the ground and they made their wobbly way to the ewe who chuckled deep in her throat as she gathered them close. Shep and Tig guided the tiny flock to the pen at Mary's command.

"Catch!" Ewan shouted a split second before he launched himself at Simon. With a startled grin, Simon caught the lad then set him on the ground. He ruffled

Ewan's hair.

"Ye are a hefty lad. How old are ye?"

"I's this many summers," Ewan replied, holding up four fingers. His thumb tried to open, and he folded it against his palm with his other hand, a look of concentration on his face.

Simon laughed. "Ye've a bit of growing to do, then." He bent close. "Keep that hair trimmed. Those curls will attract the lasses."

CHAPTER ELEVEN

S IMON HAD BEEN glad to mark the absence of Kaily's belongings when he returned to the keep later that evening. Instead of the nagging disappointment of lacking female companionship for the evening, energy raced through his veins. Enthusiastically, he detailed his plans for a second yard and outer wall, assuring each person gathered in the hall of the value of their help.

"Your men may decide to retrieve your leman if ye announce even one more task," Garin noted as men left the hall after receiving their assignments. Simon wasn't certain he joked.

"The outer wall is a necessity if we are to offer protection for the entire village. And breaking ground for various fruit trees and enlarging the gardens will please everyone once the harvest is in. The keep was left in some disorder for almost a year after we took it from the Scots, as ye well know, and I wish to make improvements. What better time than whilst we continue repairs?"

"And who will the oriel window please?" Garin nodded to the parchment beneath Simon's hand. His handwriting covered the upper portion, but a sketch of the square, tower-like keep at the bottom boasted a turret beginning approximately halfway up the outer wall which jutted out over the yard, its mullioned windows marked on the outermost wall. There was no such structure on the current keep. The beautifully detailed window seat was a marked extravagance meant to please a woman.

"That is not a matter for discussion," Simon growled. "'Twill give needed work for some craftsmen in the village. There will be times when they are not needed to watch sheep or weed gardens."

"And they will be happy to have the work." Garin pounded Simon's shoulder as he rose from the table. "Shall I send for Kaily?" Garin grinned, safe beyond Simon's reach. "Or a black-haired wench from the village with a boy tugging at her skirts?"

"'Twill be hard to replace ye after I pound ye into the ground for your insolence," Simon growled, only half-serious. He could stay as busy as a squirrel in winter, but he was unable to banish Iseabal from his mind.

"How would ye woo a lady, Garin?"

The knight halted then returned to the table. "I'm no ladies' man," he replied. "Ye are who we mere mortal men look to win a lady's attention." He shrugged. "Treat her like ye do the others. They eat from your hand readily enough."

"Therein lies my problem," Simon remarked. "I do not want her to be like the others."

⇶⇷

"When will ye tell him, lass?"

Iseabal sent Mary a wide-eyed look, halting with a half-dry mug in her hands. She cut a look to Aggie who snored softly in her chair by the hearth.

"Who?"

Mary gently took the mug and piece of linen from Iseabal's grasp and set them on the table, then led her to the pallet where Ewan slept peacefully.

"The lad's da." She shook her head. "I've naught seen another head of hair like his, all golden and tight curls, until today. With yer black hair, 'tis a wonder the lad doesnae look more like ye. But I saw the man who brought ye home, Sir Simon himself, his shiny head exactly like yer lad's." Mary waggled a finger. "If that man isnae the lad's da, then 'tis his uncle."

Iseabal's gaze lingered on Ewan. She pivoted on her heel and walked slowly to the door. She leaned against the open door frame, peering into the night. Shep left Ewan's blanket and paced to her side then flopped to his belly with a sigh and proceeded to lick his injured leg. Iseabal absently patted his head to distract him. He thumped his tail twice on the floor then resumed his slow, rhythmic treatment.

"'Tis not such a simple thing. I never thought to see him again."

Moonlight laid a silver mantle over the boulders beyond the yard. Shadows stark and black slashed across the moors, revealing dips and rills. A breeze rustled the grasses. In the distance a wolf howled.

Iseabal shuddered, remembering how close she'd come to death.

"Simon and other English knights had chased some reivers—Johnstones, I believe—across the Border at the behest of a minor English baron. Simon was injured and became separated from his men. Da forbade me to leave Eaglesmuir, warned me against the knights who wouldnae hesitate to *pluck my innocence*." One corner of her lips twitched.

"He wasnae wrong, lass," Mary said. "Ye should have listened."

"I have a problem with obedience, it seems. I rough-housed with my brother rather than attend my sewing. He taught me to use a sling—which saved my life today."

"What happed to yer brother? Why did ye not seek his protection when yer da died?"

"He drowned in the River Annan the summer I was fifteen. My sister had been sent to England to marry an English lord. My brother had always deflected the worst of Da's temper. When he died, I was all alone."

Mary clucked her tongue in sympathy.

"Walks across the moors helped put distance between me and Da. We fought less when we werenae in the same keep, so I invented reasons to be gone as much as possible. 'Twas easy to defy his order. 'Twould have been a mark of honor to capture an English knight—no matter his head had been coshed and he was near death by the time I found him."

"'Twas the charitable thing to save a man's life," Mary replied, clearly torn between hospitality and the story whose end she saw all too clearly.

"A few days' nursing care brought Simon around, though he suffered from a severe headache and blurred vision. I managed to convince him to remain in the abandoned croft a few days more—until his strength returned and I knew he could stay no longer."

The sough of the wind mesmerized Iseabal, her gaze drifting beyond the tiny yard and rough-built sheep fold. Beyond the hills and into the past.

Dinnae leave me, Simon. Tears roughened her voice. He needed her. Appreciated her. He treated her with an easy respect, teased her in a manner that left her yearning for something she did not understand.

Ye would not be happy with me, Iseabal. I am a warrior. My life is sworn to fighting.

Then fight for me! For us! Unwitting or not, he had bound her to him. To lose him was unthinkable.

Ye do not understand, my heart. I owe ye my life, and it destroys me to leave ye. Ye are beautiful, kind, and passionate. But my life is not my own to command.

She'd thrown herself at him, certain he would succumb to whatever charms she could lay claim to. She vowed she'd do *anything*, anything at all to keep her English knight.

Their lips met. He did not push her away, immediately meeting her fervor with his own. His arms wrapped about her without hesitation. Hungry glances, gentle touches, the tenderness of the past week overwhelmed by a soaring passion she'd never expected. The resulting fire had burned her, consumed her.

She'd remained the night in his arms, awakening each time he touched her, unable to resist him even when she ached with the afterglow of her arousal. Yet the morning came, and he was gone.

Iseabal breathed deep, sending the memory back to its place deep within her heart, and hazarded a glance at Mary.

The older woman's eyes told her she did not have to explain what had occurred between her and Simon. Though Mary and Clyde had been married for nearly thirty years, Iseabal had thought it sweet to see the two of them side by side, fingers entwined as they relaxed after a hard day's work. It wasn't just sweet. It was love.

"I cannae tell him," Iseabal whispered. "I cannae risk losing Ewan to him."

"He isnae married, nor betrothed, if the gossip is true—and it usually is. He has a spot in his heart for ye.

I saw how he looked at ye today."

"He may have fond memories, but 'tis not enough to get past the fact he is an English lord and I am the daughter of a bastard Scot."

"Ye dinnae think it difficult five years ago," Mary pointed out.

"He was a knight, not a landed lord."

"He would have been obliged to leave ye at whatever castle he called home for long periods of time among English ladies who would have spurned and made fun of ye. 'Tis possible he did ye a favor."

"I dinnae doubt he felt he did. That doesnae mean things would be different now."

"North Hall is his to hold for his liege. The land is his to safeguard as well. He may be called away to fight for his lord or king, but that is no longer his entire life. He has room now for a wife."

"A Scottish lass and an English lord? I pitied my sister when she was sent away to marry for the sake of peace on the Border. I must find her, though Hew gave me little hope of it."

Mary harrumphed. "Our Lady de Wylde is a lovely Scottish lass. Ye willnae find *her* suffering at Belwyck Castle. 'Tis rumored her husband is quite enamored of her."

Iseabal turned to Mary. "De Wylde? Is that not the man they call The Saint?"

"One and the same. Once the terror of the Borders, now happily being led about the moors by a wee lass with flaming hair and a disposition to match. Not that she isnae kind and sweet, mind ye, but she can hold her own against the temperamental beast."

It would be too much of a coincidence. Or was Hew's story inaccurate?

Iseabal tapped a forefinger against her lips. "When will Hew and Wil return from seeing the ewes to summer grazing?"

"Mayhap a sennight. Why?"

"I need to ask Hew about my sister."

"Yer sister?"

"Aye. He told me the last he saw of her, she had been speaking to two of The Saint's men." Her voice trailed off as realization struck. "I could ask Simon Lady de Wylde's name."

Mary waved a hand languidly in the air. "Och, 'tis simple enough. Her name is Marsaili."

SIMON GLANCED TOWARD the shout from outside the gates. Expecting a handful of village workers, he set aside his tools at the sight that trailed the pair of men demanding entrance. A party of knights, mounted atop war horses, hooves pounding the packed earth, surged up the road. Banners flew from atop poles, announcing Lord de Wylde's approach.

Simon peered in shock at the two dozen or more mounted men. Had he somehow erred? What would convince The Saint to undertake a surprise visit to North Hall? Lord de Wylde was always welcome. It was the unexpectedness that worried Simon.

He straightened his tunic and ran a palm over his hair. He reached for his short leather hauberk and pulled it over his head. Grabbing his sword and scabbard from the rock where he'd set them an hour earlier when they impeded his work, he buckled the belt about his waist then checked the placement of his daggers.

"Let them in."

He strode across the second bailey, its outline taking shape with the massive stones awaiting placement in the deep trench being dug for the footing. Timing his approach, he and six men of his guard entered the main gate moments after the de Wylde procession.

Simon glanced through the tight formation, searching for The Saint's warhorse. Instead, he came nose-to-nose with Lady de Wylde.

"My lady," he managed, concealing his surprise behind honed manners. "'Tis an honor to receive ye at North Hall." He glanced at the guards flanking her—stern-faced men in plate armor. "Might I ask the reason for your visit?"

Marsaili, red hair flaming from beneath the white veil pinned to her riotous curls, dismounted and stalked the short distance to Simon. She fisted her hands on her hips.

"I want to know what ye've done with my sister."

CHAPTER TWELVE

"KAILY TOLD ME of the lass ye brought here."

"Kaily?" Simon didn't seem to be following Lady de Wylde's words properly. "She's hardly had a chance . . . ye couldn't . . . ."

Lady de Wylde waved aside his protest. "She arrived last night and I left first thing this morn. 'Tis scarcely a morning's ride away."

"Less, if my wife is in a tear about something." Lord de Wylde stepped through the bristle of armed guards, his limp nearly gone despite the journey. But the same trip could only have been undertaken by wagon less than two months ago and Simon knew better than to mention resting the injury that had plagued the man for over a year.

"'Tis good to see ye in the saddle again, m'lord." Simon grinned. "About time to put that beastly horse of yours to doing something other than eating his head off and chasing the mares."

"Simon de Bretteby! I will have yer attention!" Marsaili's Scottish brogue broadened alongside her obvious temper. "Tell me where ye've hidden my sister or I will tear apart this keep stone by stone."

Simon knew better than to brush off Lady de Wylde. She'd earned his admiration when The Saint, Walter de Ellerton, and he had encountered her in a village miles south of the Scottish Border, berating an innkeeper for withholding a replacement to her lame mount solely because she was a woman traveling with only a single servant for protection and propriety. And she'd earned his respect when she agreed to marry The Saint. He was well aware it took a special woman to win the heart of Geoffrey de Wylde, and he'd managed to tease Lord de Wylde rather unmercifully for falling for the woman who'd tormented him most of their journey through Northern England.

"If ye would tell me your sister's name, mayhap I could be of more help to ye, m'lady."

Lady de Wylde arched a brow. "Ye have a keep so full of unattached ladies ye cannae speak for her?"

"My lady, there are mayhap a dozen ladies at North Hall. They are all spoken for, though none by me."

Marsaili stamped her foot. "I willnae be mocked.

Bring her to me this instant."

"If I knew her, I would not hesitate," Simon protested. "I swear there is not a woman here known to me as your sister. Ye are a striking woman, and though we've brunettes, blondes, and two silver-haired ladies in residence, there's not a redhead among them."

"My sister's hair is black," Marsaili retorted, "and her name is Iseabal."

»»»«««

ISEABAL GLANCED UP the hill. Beyond lay North Hall. And information about her sister. She was impatient to speak to Simon, to demand—ask—he take her to Belwyck Castle. There could scarcely be two red-haired Scottish lasses named Marsaili along the Border. The coincidence was simply too great for Lady de Wylde not to be her sister.

I am so happy ye found a man who loves ye, Marsaili. I'm sorry for the way we parted—that I dinnae understand how helpless ye were. I understand now what a sacrifice ye made, and how it kept Da satisfied for a time.

It had taken quite a while, in fact, for her da to remember he had a second daughter. Iseabal had ensured she wasn't in his presence very often once Marsaili and her brother were gone. By the time he sought to bring her to the attention of a neighboring laird's son, her belly was round with child.

Ewan.

She couldn't imagine loving anyone more. Simon was in the past, wasn't he? He'd made no advances, given her no reason to think he wished more for her than safety in Friar's Hill.

He set men to watch over her.

But he will rescind that order as soon as he determines James Maxwell is no longer a threat.

He will marry an Englishwoman of excellent blood, above reproach. Capable of running his household. Raising his children. Sharing his bed.

"Och!" Anger pricked tears behind her eyes. She wiped the back of one hand across her face before the drops could spill. "Quite a numpty ye are for pining over what ye cannae have. As soon as I've finished feeding the orphan lambs, I will march to North Hall, ask my question of his high lordship, then bid him good-day."

The sheep bleated as though in agreement, though it was much more likely they approved her decision to feed them than her declaration to walk to North Hall.

"Ma!"

Iseabal straightened, gently pushing away a lamb which grabbed a fold of her skirt and suckled heartily. Disappointed in the lack of nourishment found in the cloth, it bleated and wobbled to the ewe in the corner of the pen, likely in the hopes of managing a swallow or two before she realized he wasn't her bairn.

"Ma!" Ewan climbed up on the gate, a bannock in his hand. He waved the half-eaten oatcake. "Look! Horses!"

His excited expression slid a bit toward fear and Iseabal hastened to reassure him.

"Och, they will likely continue on to the village. Dinnae fash."

They watched as the horses ignored the rutted road to the town in favor of the rocky track to the croft.

"They're comin' here!" Ewan slipped to the ground and ran across the yard. "Aggie! Mary!"

Aggie stepped to the doorway, towel in her hands. She caught Ewan as he pelted past, slowing his headlong dash as he disappeared inside the house.

Iseabal stared at the riders. Sunlight glinted off armor and bits of dangling harness. They moved purposefully, a slender pennant snapping in the breeze. Fear exploded in Iseabal's breast. She set aside the small milk pot she'd used to feed the lambs, a wary eye on the soldiers.

"Mary!" Iseabal took a quick step toward the house, then paused.

A rider broke from the pack. The horse gathered speed and surged ahead of the others. Skirts billowed behind, a white veil rising from the rider's head.

A woman?

The veil ripped away, revealing fiery red hair. Iseabal blinked.

"Marci!"

The shriek tore from her throat. Shoving the gate open, she raced down the road. Marsaili pulled her horse to a stop and leapt to the ground. Iseabal grabbed her sister, pulling her tight as tears fell. Marsaili's arms wrapped about her.

"Izzy, Izzy!" she chanted into Iseabal's ear. Iseabal buried her face in her sister's shoulder.

Marsaili pulled back, sliding her hands down Iseabal's arms to grasp her hands. "Why are ye here? Come back with me to Belwyck Castle. I want to hear what has happened."

Iseabal shook her head. "I cannae leave. Come, walk with me and tell me everything."

A dog barked and Iseabal glanced over her shoulder. Sheep trickled in a steady line through the pen's open gate. Aggie ran from the house, waving her drying cloth in the air as she attempted to turn the sheep back.

Iseabal exchanged a guilty look with her sister and they burst into giggles. Suddenly, the past didn't matter, and Marsaili grabbed Iseabal's hand as they picked up their skirts and ran to Aggie's aid.

"Tig! Put them up!"

The young sheep, not as easily herded as the ewes would have been, kicked up their heels and scampered about the yard. Holding his injured leg against his body, Shep joined Tig, and the sheep were returned to the pen in short order. Iseabal and Marsaili collapsed onto a large boulder near the pen, breathless from their exertions.

"Young sheep Mary promised to North Hall," Iseabal gasped. "They arenae verra bright."

"No one is when they're young, Izzy," Marsaili noted with a somber note. "I'm sorry I was angry with ye when I left."

Iseabal shook her head, sobering instantly. "I din-nae stop to think what yer life would be like on the far side of the Border save for living among the English. I thought ye gave in to Da too easily. But he boasted of yer fine sacrifice for many months after, and I only knew how much I missed ye."

Marsaili patted her hand. "Especially after Ben died. I'm so sorry, Izzy. I know how close the two of ye were."

Iseabal sighed. "I dinnae know how much ye and Ben protected me until ye were both gone. But I learned to judge Da's temper and kept busy and out of his way much of the time. I managed. Da died a sennight ago after a raid at Eaglesmuir, but we'll leave that tale for later. What about ye?"

Silence filled the moment between them. Marsaili seemed to understand what a blow their da's death had dealt, even though he'd been a less than caring father. Iseabal could not bring herself to burden her sister with the harrowing assaults—on both the keep which led to Marcus's death, and on herself which had forced her to flee in the night.

Marsaili's face smoothed. "As ye said, I managed. Andrew wasnae a terrible husband, but he died a few months ago and his brother was horrid." She peered at the guards mounted nearby. "Flore had passed away a year earlier, so Hew and I escaped and headed north, intending to return to Eaglesmuir. That was a month ago, and during the worst blizzard ever! I left Hew at an inn and somewhat foolishly continued on my own. I was rescued a bit later by Geoffrey and his men, and, against my better judgement, fell in love with Geoffrey."

Her gaze moved to a large man keeping watch from atop a black war horse. "We wed nearly a month ago. I'm verra happy."

The smile on Marsaili's face completely healed Iseabal's heart. "I'm so excited for ye, Marci. Ye deserve better than Andrew."

Marsaili waved a hand airily. "Och, I daresay we both deserve to be loved, not merely used. But, why did Kaily say ye were at North Hall with Simon? Simon gave some garbled account of rescuing ye, and rain, and I dinnae stay to listen. I wanted to find ye."

Iseabal hesitated. How much should she tell her sister?

"Ma?"

Ewan halted at her side and placed a small hand on

her skirt. Iseabal stared into his green eyes and smoothed a hand over his wind-blown curls. A smile curved her lips and she turned to Marsaili. Her sister stared at Ewan, eyes wide.

"Oh, Iseabal. He looks like Simon!" Her look of surprise turned to Iseabal. "Ye arenae wed? Simon isnae wed." Her jaw shut audibly and she shook her head. "I need to hear this, Izzy."

"'Twas foolishness. He dinnae . . . ." She sent Marsaili a pointed look, a nod to Ewan.

Marsaili cupped Ewan's chin in her palm. "Be a good laddie and run and tell Mary I'll be stayin' for a bit o' bread and cider. The men can fend for themselves, so dinnae fash."

Ewan nodded. Marsaili held up a single finger. "Only one extra plate, remember. That's a good lad."

Ewan darted back to the house.

Marsaili perched on the boulder as if prepared to remain as long as it took to hear Iseabal's confession.

"Now. Tell me everything. When did ye meet Simon . . .?" Her eyes widened. "Och, he told me he'd been to Lockardebi. The *radgie* scoundrel! 'Twas *ye* he met there!"

"Da and some of his billies got caught reiving and

they were chased back across the Border by knights sent by Lord de Wylde. Simon was injured and I hid him in that old tumble-down croft until he healed." Iseabal rolled a strip of her skirt beneath her fingers.

"He was quite well when he left."

"He left a bairn in yer belly," Marsaili noted. "Though I daresay he never knew. Young Ewan's got the Maxwell brow and yer green eyes, but he has Simon's golden curls."

Iseabal's stomach dropped. "Mary noticed, as well. I worry what will happen if Simon finds out. I've no place else to go."

"What nonsense! Ye will stay with me at Belwyck Castle if necessary. Howbeit, if ye've a modicum of sense in yer head, ye will tell Simon straight away."

"Nae! He cannae know!"

"He isnae daft. He will work out the truth soon enough. Better an accord between ye than anger. Besides, he is honorable and will take ye and his son in."

"I dinnae want him to take us in! I want to be left alone."

Marsaili snapped her fingers beneath Iseabal's nose.

"Ye'll listen to me, Izzy Maxwell. Yer lad, as adorable as he is, is a bastard. Ye know how being known as such tormented Da. Is that what ye wish for Ewan? Decisions and chances taken from him because of his birth?"

Iseabal stiffened. "It doesnae have to be that way. Everyone here believes I am widowed. None need know differently."

"So, ye'll raise him on yer own? Here? To be a shepherd? When he could be a nobleman's son?"

"Stop! I dinnae wish to marry Simon."

"Ye have no family other than me. No one to protect ye, for I dinnae expect Lord de Wylde to side with ye in any decisions regarding Simon. Ye will wed one day. Do ye wish Ewan to be at the mercy of a man who may not accept raising another man's son?"

Iseabal gritted her teeth. "I willnae be forced to marry."

Marsaili laid a gentling hand on Iseabal's forearm. "Dearest sister, think of Ewan. 'Tis not as if I'm recommending ye marry a total stranger, or a man who will cause ye harm. Simon is a good man."

"I know he wouldnae harm me intentionally. But I have changed. And Simon is now a stranger to me."

"Izzy, good marriages often begin with less. Please think on it. Howbeit, if ye cannae commend yerself to marriage, rest assured ye are always welcome at Belwyck with me."

"As yer companion?" Iseabal managed a wry grin.

"Aye. And to give Ewan a brighter future."

CHAPTER THIRTEEN

S IMON STARED AT the mug on his desk. How on earth could he have missed the lasses' resemblance? That one sister was a fiery redhead and the other's hair was black as night should not have made a difference. Those eyes! He shook his head, tempted to pour another cup of ale to assuage his confusion, but lost interest as his thoughts returned to Iseabal.

How was I supposed to know? He stood, the unsatisfactory interview with Marsaili still chaffing.

What does it matter? Her relationship to Lady de Wylde makes no difference to me. Even after five years it appears I have not forgotten my sweet Scottish lass, and I care not whose sister she is.

He crossed the room, arms folded behind him, to stand at the narrow window. Horses milled about in the yard. Marsaili and The Saint had returned. Cook would produce a meal adequate for their guests, Lady de Wylde would likely prattle on about her sister, and they would be gone in the morning.

After which, he would seek out Iseabal Maxwell himself.

"Sir Simon."

He turned. Iseabal stood in the doorway.

"Ye need not call me Sir," he murmured, drinking in the sight. The past five years had been kind to her, rounding her figure in a manner which pleased his eye, made his palms itch and his cock take notice. She possessed an air of maturity. Solemnity had replaced the carelessness of youth—which he found he regretted. He wondered if the passion they'd once shared still existed. Her black hair shone, the tip of her braid hanging below her hips. He remembered the weight of it, the thick strands like silk running through his fingers.

He cleared his dry throat and motioned to the lone chair by the hearth. "Please come in. Shall I have refreshments sent in?"

Iseabal crossed the room and stood next to the fire, her hands wrinkling her skirt in a nervous gesture.

"I dinnae believe I could eat a bite just now."

Simon raised his eyebrows, not understanding, but determined to encourage her. "I see. Then have a seat and tell me what I may do for ye."

She looked away. "This is difficult. For several reasons." With a small huff, either for courage or to firm her decision, she lifted her chin and gazed at him.

"I must introduce someone to ye. Introduce him properly, that is." She motioned to the door. Lady de Wylde stepped just inside, Iseabal's son before her.

Marsaili gave the boy a gentle nudge, sending him to Iseabal. "I'll be just outside, Izzy."

Iseabal nodded once, her skin pale.

Simon couldn't resist. "Izzy?"

Color rose in Iseabal's cheeks. He liked that, so he said it again. "Izzy."

Her eyes flashed. "Only my sister calls me that. Ye may not."

He didn't mind the rebuke. He'd gotten her mind off whatever was worrying her—at least for a moment. He'd do it again if necessary.

Iseabal placed her palms on the boy's shoulders, holding him before her. "Ye saw Ewan the night we arrived, and again yesterday. But I dinnae introduce him properly. Ye . . . asked about his da."

Something bothered Simon about the hesitance in her voice. "Ye said his father rode to fight with the

English and never returned."

"Aye. 'Tis true. Though somewhat misleading. He fought *with* the English, not *against* them. And 'tis true he never returned. I was never told what happened to him, and 'twas easier to allow people to believe his da had died."

Simon stared at the boy, his wide brow and green eyes exactly like his mother's. His hair, however, was bright golden blond with curls much like . . . .

Simon dragged his gaze to Iseabal, shock seared deep into his soul.

"Ewan is my son."

Iseabal nodded, silent. Simon crossed the short distance between them. Cupping Iseabal's cheeks between his palms, he tilted her face up and lowered his lips to hers. She startled but did not pull away. He slowly broke the kiss, the taste of her lingering on his tongue, as perfect as he remembered.

"I am sorry for what my actions cost ye, Iseabal. I'm a man grown, and know of ways to keep from siring a child, though such things are not always effective."

He placed his hand atop Ewan's head, marveling at the boy.

"My son."

Simon couldn't have hidden his grin if he'd tried.

"I'm very glad I had the chance to love ye, Iseabal. Very glad. We will wed as soon as the documents can be drawn up."

Iseabal turned Ewan about. "Go with Auntie Marci," she urged. "I will come find ye in a bit."

Ewan nodded, a wary eye on Simon, then edged from the room.

"Simon, I dinnae bring Ewan here to force a proposal from ye. I have lain awake at night, worried ye would take him from me if ye knew he is yer son. Ye have power and I have none. Though ye would be within yer rights to claim him, I have no wish to marry ye."

"I have lain awake, also, Iseabal. But 'twas because I'd encountered a green-eyed beauty on the road to the village three days ago whom I'd once thought lost to me. I will not take Ewan from ye. However, our marriage is in his best interest, also, and though ye seem certain I would be a poor husband for ye, I swear I will be a good father to Ewan."

"He is doing fine with Aggie and me."

With an effort, Simon crushed his rising temper. "I

will not stand by and see my son raised to be a shepherd, outside the privilege and position I can give him. I would have him be more than my bastard son."

ISEABAL WRUNG HER hands. Why had she allowed Marci to sway her?

"I have been offered a position at Belwyck. 'Twill be a good place for both of us. Protection, a roof over our heads. 'Tis not so far away ye cannae see Ewan from time to time. And Ewan will be able to obtain an education there."

"I can provide for my own son, Iseabal," Simon growled, eyebrows snapping together.

Iseabal's heart raced. As she feared, he would not give in. Yet, succumbing to marriage without a bond between them brought her nigh to tears. By Saint Columba's bones, she'd had enough of living as others expected. She'd suffered through the disgrace of being an unwed mother, of birthing a fatherless child. Everything she did was to Ewan's benefit. She'd earned the right to the man of her choice.

Unless she fled Friar's Hill, there was little she could do. And she was certain they could not travel fast enough or far enough to evade Simon's reach.

"I simply dinnae wish to marry for the sake of charity."

"This is not charity, Iseabal. If I did not wish to marry ye, I would not ask it. Ye have offered me a great gift—knowledge of my son. I *want* ye to marry me, and mayhap give me a daughter with yer black hair and passion for life."

Iseabal bit her lip, his request striking a chord deep inside. A daughter—like her? He wanted her in his bed, 'twas plain to see, for his trim, laced breeches left little to her imagination. Her skin heated beneath his gaze. She could speak a lie to say she did not want him. But would either of them believe it?

"We are different. Ye're English!" she blurted, tossing out her finest defense.

To her surprise, he grinned. "I was an English knight when ye seduced me. It didn't bother ye then."

"Och, it took a full day to decide not to turn ye over to my da," Iseabal retorted, stung that he would laugh at her youthful indiscretion.

Simon caught her braid in one hand and drew it over her shoulder, the motion slow and sensual. "And how long did it take for ye to fall in love with me, sweet Izzy?"

She faltered. Her heart raced. "Three days," she whispered. Three days after she'd met him, she was certain she could not live without him.

"Give me three days to win your heart again."

>>>><<<<

"IT FEELS DECEITFUL," Iseabal sighed. She set a platter of cheese and dried apples on the table before Ewan and filled his mug with watered ale. Popping a bite of sharp cheese into her mouth, she chewed and swallowed before sitting next to her sister at the long table.

"If I refuse Simon's proposal, he will believe I'm using his son as leverage, though for the life of me I dinnae know what I would ask of him." Her shoulders fell. "Och, Marci, would Simon even have noticed me were it not for Ewan?"

Marsaili grinned, her eyes dancing, and Iseabal considered storming off in a huff, not in the least enjoying her sister's obvious glee at her expense.

"Ye must have some feelings left for him, Izzy. He's a good man, well made, and willing to give ye whatever ye ask."

"I . . . ." Iseabal frowned.

"Ye want love and fear he only offers security."

Marsaili tilted her head. "Many women have neither."

"I know. 'Tis unreasonable. Yet, I remember how it once was between us. No more than a sennight, yet 'twill be stamped on my soul forever."

"'Twas good ye decided to tell him of Ewan. He appeared absolutely delighted when he ushered ye from his solar, Izzy. He still has feelings for ye."

"He calls me *Izzy* now, Marci." She rolled her eyes. "Your fault."

Marsaili waggled her fingers dismissively. "Och, ye dinnae mind *me* calling ye Izzy. And I'm not always nice about it."

Ewan drained his mug and set it on the table with a thump. "I finished, Ma."

"Well done," Iseabal said, seizing the opportunity to take action.

"I cannae do this, Marci. 'Tis best we leave." She gathered Ewan and rose from the table. Brushing crumbs from his tunic onto the trencher, she pointed him toward the door.

"We've imposed on Sir Simon long enough. 'Tis time to return home. Aggie will have supper ready, and 'twill soon be yer bedtime."

"I wanna see Da," Ewan said, avoiding Iseabal's

reach and heading toward the solar.

"Little pitchers have big ears," Marsaili mocked.

"Saint Ninian's toes!" Iseabal muttered, aghast Ewan had understood her conversation with Simon. She dashed after Ewan, catching him several feet from the door.

"Dinnae fash, my wee *nacket*. Sir Simon is a busy man and we will see him another day."

Ewan dropped to his haunches, breaking again from Iseabal's grasp, this time to squat mutinously on the floor.

"I dinnae wanna go!"

"Haud ye wheesht, Ewan," Iseabal scolded. "'Tis no way for ye to act. Ye will come home with me now."

"No!"

The door to Simon's solar opened.

"What manner of ruckus are ye creating, young Ewan?" Simon's voice held steady, though his expression demanded the lad cease his caterwauling.

Ewan glanced up from his undignified spot on the floor. "I wanna see ye."

Simon sent Iseabal a questioning look. She drew what dignity she could about her.

"'Tis growing late and the lad needs his supper and

bed. We wish to return home."

Ewan shook his head in disagreement. Simon arched a brow, matching the gesture with a curved lip as he stepped close to Iseabal and tucked a strand of hair behind her ear.

"Ye wouldn't cheat me out of my three days, would ye?"

A shiver of desire shot through Iseabal before she could steel herself against the reaction. Simon leaned closer, the heat of his body overwhelming, his nearness both a frustration and a delight. Liquid heat softened Iseabal's bones as Simon kissed her ear.

"Do not forget, my heart. Ye *are* home."

"I dinnae say we would wed."

"Ye will."

Torn between laughter and outrage, Iseabal planted a fist on one hip. "Ye cannae force me into marriage, Simon de Bretteby."

He caught her hand and drew it to his lips, dropping a kiss to the backs of her fingers. Her skin sizzled. "I do not plan to force ye, Izzy. Persuasion is a much finer tool."

CHAPTER FOURTEEN

WITH A NARROW look, Simon answered Garin's silent request to join him in the lord's solar. He trusted his captain realized the poor timing as he apologized to Iseabal and crossed to the small room, Lord de Wylde at his side.

"Found him knocking at the gate like a proper gentleman. As he was alone, the guard allowed him in." Garin nodded to a disreputable man standing in the middle of the room. "Says his name is Henry. He's a Scot."

With a bob of his head, the man offered a placating smile.

Simon examined the wizened Scot with a wary eye. Lord de Wylde stood half in shadow in a corner of the small room, observing, offering neither command nor suggestion. The change in authority from The Saint was not lost on Simon, and marked Simon's rise in rank. Simon was lord at North Hall and this was not

Lord de Wylde's business.

He transferred his attention to the old Scot. "Why should I trust ye?"

The old man, his gray hair unkempt, clothes tattered and in desperate need of a wash—or immolation—shrugged, his gaze traveling to the flask on the low table.

"I overheard two men in the tavern. I was sober, ye ken? Nary a bit of coin to pay for a shot o' whisky." He tilted his head in a hopeful manner.

"He's known in the village," Garin said, his stance close to the elderly Scot protecting both Simon and Lord de Wylde. "Harmless."

"That's me," the old man agreed with a gap-toothed grin. "Harmless Henry. Nae one pays heed to Harmless Henry."

Simon sent Garin a nod. The flask clanked against the mug's rim as Garin poured a finger of whisky. Henry licked his lips, eyes glowing. He accepted the mug and took a sip, holding the spirits in his mouth a moment before he swallowed. He sighed and his eyes drifted closed.

"Peat. Driftwood. A hint of salty sea spray." His eyes flashed with a wink. "Could cure the ills of the world, it could."

"Tell me what ye overheard." Despite the Scotsman's unexpected accurate assessment of the lowland whisky, Simon brought him back to the reason he'd arrived at the keep an hour earlier.

Henry tipped the mug up, draining the last drop, releasing a slow gasp of pleasure. He wiped his lips with the back of a hand. "Auld man Johnstone's wife, the one whose sheep ye saved from the reivers? Mistress Johnstone recognized the pair o' ruffians in the middle of the village, bold as brass." He held up his empty mug in a hopeful gesture.

Simon did not budge. "When ye've finished and I'm satisfied with your report."

Henry shrugged. "She was in a dither. 'Tis likely the entire village has heard of 'em by now. But none brave enough to take 'em on and send 'em on their way."

"What did ye hear?"

"I followed 'em to the tavern, heard they was lookin' fer their fellows what dinnae make it home t' other night. Hopin' someone'd taken 'em in, though after creatin' such a stramash, I dinnae ken why they'd think we would."

Henry shrugged again, as if he'd encountered

enough people who defied his definition of intelligent to easily place these two on the list.

"Nary a *gleg* thought betwixt them, if ye ask me. So, I pointed out their error and gave 'em the direction of the kirkyard to find their wayward laddies. They seemed a bit disturbed. Mayhap even riled."

Simon strode to the door and spoke to the guard standing in the hall. "Take Henry to the hall and feed him. Have Alane find him suitable clothing, then send him back to the village." He cast a brief look at the Scot. "Keep an eye on him."

The guard stepped to the doorway and beckoned to Henry. Garin offered the flask and the old man beamed with delight, his cloth-bound feet making shushing sounds on the stone as he quit the room, the whisky tucked beneath his tattered cloak.

Simon folded his arms over his chest and glanced at his captain. "Do ye believe they'll take the hint we will not suffer reiving and return to Eaglesmuir a bit wiser? Or should we place a guard in the village until this is sorted out?"

Garin's lips drew together in a fine line. "We've enough men to spare for the village, and coin to spread about for further word." His face cleared and a wry look brightened his eyes. "Since ye've brought your Scottish lass to the keep, her guard is no longer about."

"Yes," Lord de Wylde drawled. "My wife has been most delighted with your decision. I'll have to hear the story of how ye and her sister met sometime soon. And, I agree, the men can now be used elsewhere."

"Send them to watch the shepherd's croft where she lived."

"Lived?" Lord de Wylde's eyebrows rose.

"She will be my wife inside the week." Simon's grin matched Garin's. "She'll not live in a croft again."

⇒⇒⇒⇐⇐⇐

ISEABAL FROWNED IN indecision and drew her fingers through Ewan's thick curls. "I've never been away from him before."

"And I've never spent time with him," Marsaili countered. "'Tis only for a few days, and we've sent for Aggie to come with us. He'll be around people who love him, and a familiar face in case he gets a bit homesick. Dinnae fash. We'll return in time for the wedding."

Iseabal tilted her head in warning. "I dinnae wish to rush into this. I dinnae fall in love with a nobleman five years ago. I fell in love with a man who took notice of me, touched me kindly, and made me laugh." Her gaze fell upon the closed door to the lord's solar. "I fear he no longer has time for me."

"I vow he will make time for ye, Sister. But ye are nae longer a child and cannae expect all of his attention all of the time. Decide how ye mean to live yer life and dinnae dither about."

"Words of wisdom from my elder sister who has been lucky enough to find the love of her life."

"I will love ye no matter what ye decide. Geoffrey has agreed ye are to come to Belwyck Castle if ye dinnae marry Simon. Though he said *aye* with a brief shrug that indicates he doesnae truly believe ye'll come." Marsaili's eyes twinkled. "Now, go give Simon a chance, and dinnae worry about wee Ewan. I'll see to it he's cared for properly and kept busy."

"If I agree, will ye promise not to give him a pony?"

The door to the solar opened and a wizened man hobbled out, guided to a corner of the hall by a guard. A moment later, Lord de Wylde, Garin, and Simon strolled into the room. Ewan abandoned his toys and bolted from the rug near the hearth.

"Da!"

Iseabal's heart thudded at the gleeful sound of Ewan's voice. She shared a hesitant look with Marsaili. Her sister shrugged, a smug grin on her face.

"I dinnae have to promise. Simon has already given him one."

Iseabal startled. "He cannae . . . ."

"Och, aye, he can. But dinnae fash. Geoffrey assures me the pony is sturdy and kind, and has raised a number of children. He's a fat beast, and the village baker drove a hard bargain."

Marsaili touched Iseabal's hand. "Simon deserves a lass like ye who will love him, not a calculating witch like Kaily, who, for all her beauty, cannae see beyond her next gown. Give him a chance."

"I've always said your sister has a bright head upon her shoulders," Simon commented as he completed the distance to Iseabal, clearly close enough to hear her words. Ewan bounced upon Simon's broad shoulders, scarcely enough weight to bother a man used to chain mail and armor.

From his great height, Ewan sent Iseabal a shy look. "Da!" he said, patting Simon's head.

"And I'm your Uncle Geoffrey," Lord de Wylde interjected, reaching up for Ewan. The lad hesitated then held his arms out, leaning trustingly to the other man. "Ye are coming with us for a day or two, and Aggie will tag along to be certain ye eat your vegetables."

Ewan wrinkled his face and settled onto Lord de Wylde's shoulders. "Pony! Let's go!" He tugged Geoffrey's longer hair as though the dark strands were reins.

"Ow!" Lord de Wylde gave a mighty shake, his hands firm on the boy's legs to keep from dislodging him. Ewan shrieked with laughter.

Geoffrey sent Iseabal a pained look. "Make your decision fast. I'm not certain we'll survive for long at the hands of Master Ewan."

Iseabal's heart filled to overflowing. She'd never been surrounded by such loving acceptance in her life. Rather than attempt to pressure or shame her into marrying Ewan's father, they treated her, Ewan, and Simon to good-natured teasing, as if she had complete control over the matter.

It was a lie, but she loved them for giving her a bit of the dignity she'd bartered away five years ago.

By the time Ewan's belongings were gathered and he'd met—and Iseabal had approved—his new pony,

Aggie arrived, Shep with her. The dog and the plump pony, whom Ewan promptly named Bausie, sniffed noses and instantly became friends, Shep crouching at Bausie's flank while the crowd mounted and said their good-byes.

With a tingle of wariness, anticipation, and something she couldn't quite identify, Iseabal edged against Simon as his arm slid about her waist. The strength of his body, the gentle pressure of his hand, and the confidence of his possessive gesture reassured her. As did the low rumble of his voice.

"I am glad ye agreed to allow Ewan to spend the next few days with your sister. He will be safe at Belwyck Castle. I am anxious to get to know him better, but I am also anxious to give us time together as well."

"I dinnae wish there to be regret between us. I dinnae wed any of the lads my da tried to force on me because I knew they offered marriage for reasons other than me."

"Ye are a strong woman. I like that about ye."

Simon urged her forward, and they strolled across the bailey and through the gates. Sunlight glinted off the de Wylde knights' armor and harnesses several lengths ahead. With a glance and a nod to the guards at the gate, Simon continued to a small burn that bubbled beside the road. Finally, they halted, and he braced a booted foot upon a large rock.

"Tell me how ye got here," he said. "Why ye traveled at night to arrive at Friar's Hill with naught more than a boy, his nurse, and an old man at your side."

"And a dog. Dinnae forget Shep." Iseabal couldn't resist the tease, though she belatedly remembered Shep had bitten one of Simon's knights.

"He did his best to protect ye," Simon agreed. "Though hardly enough to count him as enough protection for your journey."

Iseabal perused the burn as she sorted through her thoughts. The gurgle of water soothed her. She pulled her cloak from her shoulders, enjoying the warmth of the sun. Simon took her cloak and draped it over a boulder.

"My da wasnae an easy man. Aggie had been after me for some time to leave Eaglesmuir—and him—and come here where her sister lives. I knew 'twas a good decision, but 'twas difficult to abandon all I knew." She ducked her head. "No matter how bad, he was all the family I had left."

Simon touched her cheek, tilted her face up, and gently kissed her lips. He held her gaze until she gave a small nod of understanding.

I am your family. Ye are mine.

"When Da was caught reiving, English knights were sent to punish him. He holed up in Eaglesmuir until the walls fell. A large stone struck him, and though he lingered for more than a sennight, he died.

"As he lay dying, our people left the keep. 'Tis difficult to admit he wasnae popular even with his own people, but by the time he passed, only a handful remained. A few returned for his funeral, but 'twas only the four of us that eve when Albert and James Maxwell arrived to take over the keep."

"James Maxwell is the one I caught attempting to steal sheep the night ye arrived in Friar's Hill."

"Aye. And a more *daupit* man I've never encountered." A faint smile tilted her lips as she realized the portent of her words. "And I've known my fair plenty."

"We captured two of his men that night." Simon's voice, tight and drawn, tested her reaction.

"I know. I couldnae believe they'd followed me this far . . . ."

"They did not follow ye. They were after sheep. Do

not feel guilty for their deaths."

Iseabal blinked back tears. "The world is often cruel. I cannae claim responsibility for everyone's mistakes."

"No. But mayhap ye and I together can weather what storms come our way. Mayhap create some things to rejoice over."

Iseabal's smile returned. "'Tis only the first day, Sir Simon. Or did ye mean to cheat me of my three days?"

CHAPTER FIFTEEN

S IMON CAUGHT ISEABAL'S hands and drew her close. "I most certainly am not planning on losing a moment of the next three days." He cupped her face in his palms. "I do, howbeit, plan on cheating whenever the opportunity arises."

Iseabal's heartbeat spiked as he slowly lowered his lips to hers. The scent of something spicy that was all Simon filled her senses. The taste of whisky warmed her as his tongue parted her lips, drawing the intimacy deeper.

A hum of approval fluttered in Iseabal's throat unbidden, her body instantly recalling the passion that had once flared between them and set her aflame. She leaned against him, pressing her breasts against his solid chest, her belly cradling the rigid proof of his desire.

His hands slid to her shoulders and forward, caressing her breasts, lifting them, thumbs stroking her nipples into hard peaks that ached for his touch.

Iseabal gasped, her attention instantly drawn from the thorough exploration of her mouth, to heat spiking in her belly. Her breasts filled his hands, strained against the cloth of her dress.

Simon's hands dropped to her waist. He ended the kiss, placing his forehead against hers as his breathing slowed. He straightened.

"We should return to the keep."

Iseabal startled, aware of the bodice of her dress slanting off one shoulder, her hair sliding from its braid and hanging about her face. Cheating or not, this was moving faster than she was ready for. Marci and Ewan were scarcely out of sight and he proposed to return to the keep—why? He'd promised three days of wooing, and it had been perhaps three minutes. She was not ready to stumble into his bed. Stubbornness reared its head.

She drew back, straightening her bodice. "I dinnae believe . . . ."

A slight frown crossed his face and she realized his attention was not on her, but on the wooded area some distance away. He glanced at her and flashed a smile. Meant to reassure, but it sent Iseabal's heart racing again as he drew her against his side.

Danger. They were in danger.

"Ewan," she breathed, her throat tight with dread.

Simon's chuff of laughter startled her.

"My heart, did ye not see the men Ewan rides with? 'Twill take more than Scottish reivers to put our child in danger." He tucked a lock of her hair behind one ear and she patted it absently into place.

Iseabal's mind whirled. Seeing the truth of Ewan's safety. Simon's alert telling her Scottish reivers were in the area—could it be James Maxwell?

Hearing the affirmation Ewan was *our child*. Not hers alone, nor his to take from her. But *their* child. To raise together, should she agree to his proposal.

"There will come a time when this, too, will be protected from attack." He nodded to the land immediately around them and Iseabal slid from her musings to note the beginnings of a second wall. "This will be large enough for all the villagers, should the need arise. But until then, 'tis safer inside the keep."

Simon grasped her hand and led her the short distance back through the gates. He halted as Garin strode toward them.

"Promise me ye will not leave these gates again

without either myself or a guard I have given ye."

Conscious of the men on the wall who observed everything with interest—including what had just occurred outside the walls—Iseabal nodded, her cheeks heating.

THE BLUSH ON Iseabal's cheeks was becoming, giving her pale skin a hint of the intimacy they'd shared moments ago. Hell, everything about her intrigued him, fueled a passion he'd all but forgotten. Kaily and her predecessors had met a need he'd mistaken for an appetite which could be indulged but never sated.

Until now. He'd not made love to her, scarcely touched her beyond a kiss—though the kiss had startled him with how quickly it flared beyond his control—yet his hunger for her defied a simple toss in bed. He wanted her, wanted to love her, protect her. Never let her out of his sight again. He would give everything he owned to make her smile—and to plant another bairn in her belly.

Three days. He had three days to win her heart again. From her response he'd little doubt he'd accomplish the feat, but he wanted her complete attention. Worry over Ewan was the last thing she needed. He could take that trouble from her.

"Ewan is in good hands. Ye know this, do ye not?"

"Aye. I trust my sister to have his best interests at heart, and I trust yer liege lord to keep Ewan safe." She placed her fingertips against the front of his tunic. "And I trust ye wouldnae allow our son to come to harm."

His heart beat erratically beneath her touch, pounded pridefully at her acknowledgement Ewan was his son as much as he was hers. Oh, yes, he certainly looked forward to another bairn.

He bent and kissed her again, brief but pulling away reluctantly, letting her know how much he enjoyed the embrace, stopping before the kiss could become more intimate—though it was harder than he'd imagined, even with Garin only a few steps away. Letting her know that he respected her too much to create a spectacle, yet unafraid to claim her as his.

He gripped her hand, twining his fingers with hers, keeping her firmly at his side as he shifted to hear what Garin had to say.

The big man halted and gave Iseabal a respectful nod.

"M'lady." He turned to Simon. "M'lord. Cook has

requested an interview at your earliest convenience."

Simon tilted his gaze to Iseabal, deferring to her. "My lady?"

"Of course. Dinnae fash over me. I will find something else to do." She wiggled her fingers, but he squeezed back, not releasing her hand.

Simon crooked a finger beneath her chin, tilting her face to meet his gaze. "I will certainly need your help, my heart."

She sent him a puzzled glance, then nodded. They walked to the hall, Simon pointing out structures along the way. Not that he sensed a burning desire in her to acknowledge the smithy or weaponry—though she did show interest in the stables, which he filed away for later—but he found he enjoyed having her at his side. He was proud of his improvements to the keep, and being able to share his accomplishments and plans with her paired with the added pleasure in involving her and receiving her approval.

Word of his interest in Iseabal and subsequent proposal must have traveled fast, for when they reached the hall, soldiers and servants nodded or bowed respectfully, their gazes lingering curiously on Iseabal. Her warm smile as she recognized each of them boded well for her future as lady of North Hall, and Simon grinned.

Cook was a woman of middle years, dark hair mostly hidden beneath a kerchief, a twinkle in her eye, and a Scottish brogue as broad as the waistline her apron strings struggled to contain.

"I'm in need of yer preferences fer the banquet, m'lord," she reminded him. "A weddin' feast takes some time to prepare. I willnae have it said Rhona dinnae do her duty by her lordship."

Iseabal's eyes flew wide. Simon allowed a tiny edge of his amusement of her reaction to show and tucked her hand along his forearm, forestalling a potential bolt by his skittish bride-to-be.

"My lady has not yet granted my request," he drawled. "Never fear. This banquet will see her into the future of her choice."

The reassurance seemed to mollify both Iseabal and Rhona.

Cook sniffed. "She's a right comely lass and anyone can see why yer smitten with her." She eyed Simon. "And there's times when a Scottish lass could do worse than take an English lord as husband."

Simon blinked, sifting through Cook's words to

determine if she spoke a compliment or insult. His teeth showed in a slow grin of admiration.

"If I have need of a voice on my council, would ye accept?"

"I am free to choose my alliances," Cook reminded him. "Howbeit, I willnae betray one fer another."

"Would ye approve this marriage?"

"If 'tis her heart's desire, I would defend it." Cook cracked a smile. "Though I'd be careful should ye betray her heart."

"A threat?"

Cook waggled a finger and raised a brow. "Nae, a warning to an impetuous English lord who enjoys a full belly."

"I like, ye, Rhona. I hope my lady does as well." Impressed as he was with the new cook of North Hall, Simon wanted Iseabal to understand she had the right to build her own staff should she find any lacking.

ISEABAL SMOTHERED A smile. She'd found an ally within the hall and wondered what Rhona would spice Simon's food with should she ever believe he trifled with her heart. It pleased her Rhona did not judge Simon or their potential marriage solely based on culture or which side of the Border they had been born. As Iseabal was coming to learn, love wasn't about boundaries, but rather their lack.

How to give someone the freedom to choose their future without the strictures of reminding them of the past? She'd put her love for Simon in a box of youthful expectations, anguished when he was unable to change to fit. Had she hated him when she discovered she was pregnant with Ewan? No. Hated that her plans had fallen so far, despaired of the path she'd chosen. But it had been her decision more than Simon's, though she'd been unaware at the time how much his leaving her had cost him. Her only consideration had been how much his leaving had cost *her*.

She turned a thoughtful gaze to Sir Simon Bretteby, now Lord of North Hall. His profile, chiseled and fine, had aged a bit. Time had etched fine lines at the corners of his eyes, and a thin white scar traced the angle of his jaw. But his eyes met hers with a twinkle and his lips turned up in soft humor.

He's always treated me fairly. I've never known judgement or criticism at his hand.

He offers me security, respectability—and love?

Her lips tingled. Oh, there was that, as well. Mayhap more likely passion, but where does the boundary between passion and love lie?

"I will leave ye but a moment to see to the menu with Cook." Simon kissed the backs of her fingers. "I will return."

Iseabal nodded, her heart giving a peculiar thud as he strode away.

"M'lady?" Cook cleared her throat.

"I believe I like ye, as well, Rhona," Iseabal said. "Let's see to the menu."

Cook had the plans well in hand, and Iseabal had little to remark. She learned Simon enjoyed roasted quail, but not redressed peacock.

"He said he'd sooner not eat as to be reminded of the death of such a beautiful bird, though during mating season, I'd likely strangle the lot o' 'em myself, as noisy as they are," Cook confided. She glanced about. "Men. I've me work cut out fer me and nary a sign of m'lord."

"Dinnae fash over me," Iseabal protested with a wave of her hand. "I've been looking after myself for a number of years. I'm nae dependent on m'lord now."

"Good to hear," Cook replied. "Though I'll not leave ye at loose ends." She caught a passing young woman, her arms laden with a platter of bread and cheese for the hall.

"Rosaline will keep ye company until m'lord returns."

Rosaline placed her platter on a nearby table and gave a brief curtsy. "M'lady."

Iseabal was struck by the young woman's closed face, neither friendly nor hostile. No mischief lurked in the sad violet eyes.

"I'm pleased to see ye again, Rosaline. Come walk with me and tell me about North Hall."

CHAPTER SIXTEEN

S IMON HALTED IN the entry to the hall, astonished at how hungry he was for the sight of Iseabal. And how much he'd feared she wouldn't be in the hall when he returned. But she was, her raven hair gleaming with sunlight shining through the window slit high in the wall. She appeared in deep conversation with one of the servants—a young woman with red-gold hair Walter had once shown an interest in. He couldn't remember her name, but it didn't seem to matter.

He crossed to the table, smiling as Iseabal glanced up, the sparkle of welcome in her eyes. Sending a nod of dismissal to the serving girl, he presented Iseabal with a handful of flowers. She reached for them slowly with a shy tilt of her head.

"This is the important matter?" She held the yellow blossoms to her nose, inhaling their sweet scent.

"Naught is more important than finding something which makes my lady smile," Simon replied. "The keep will run itself for the next three days."

"Or with Sir Garin's intervention," Iseabal suggested. Again, the pleased sparkle in her eyes warmed his heart clear down to his toes and sent heat streaking to his cock. He stared at her as though she was an apparition who would soon vanish.

Abruptly, he held a hand out. "Come with me. I have years to catch up on."

He led her to his solar, closing the door behind them as they entered the cozy room. A peat fire smoldered on the hearth, nicely balancing the cool spring breezes drifting through the narrow window.

Simon took the flowers and laid them on the desk, then pulled Iseabal into his embrace. She leaned gently against him, tilting her face to receive his kiss. He accepted her offer, answering with a hunger that roared from deep inside. His hands filled with the weight of her breasts, and his groin tightened at the moan that tore from her throat.

Iseabal had never held herself from him. Not as an inexperienced young woman of sixteen summers, and not now, five years later. She was neither coy nor prudish, and he would have spread her across his desk, her skirts lifted about her waist if the clash of steel outside the window hadn't pushed through the fog in his brain.

He stiffened, lifting his head, alert to danger. A shout of male laughter rumbled and steel rang again.

Practice. In the yard.

But the interruption cooled his ardor somewhat, or at least drove it to a manageable state. He forced his lips into a slight smile—perhaps grimace was a better description. The pain from his denied cock was slow to settle.

"I have no willpower where ye are concerned. I hope ye do not mind if Ewan spends a bit of time with your sister and his nurse whilst we become accustomed to one another."

Iseabal raised a brow, her green eyes sparking. "How long do ye suppose it will take before we ... before it doesnae ...." She shrugged helplessly, her fingertips stroking the front of his tunic as if she was loath to stop touching him.

"If we're lucky, mayhap never," he replied. "Yet I'm willing to risk it."

Tempting himself with one last kiss, he then seated Iseabal before the hearth before dragging his chair from behind his desk. He placed it next to her, facing away, and straddled the seat, forearms resting on the high back.

"Tell me about Ewan. I want to know everything. Was he an early babe? Big? Small? When did he walk? Speak? What was his first word?"

Iseabal laughed, easing Simon's tension. He could tell she was pleased with his questions about their son, but his curiosity went far deeper.

Tell me what I need to hear about Ewan. Tell me he reminded ye of me every single day. Tell me ye do not regret his birth.

"Ye may ask questions one at a time," she teased. "I cannae keep up with ye otherwise."

"Will ye answer me simply?" he countered.

"Nae," she breathed, her love for the lad shining from her face. "I'll likely blather on until supper if ye dinnae halt my words."

Simon eyed her lips, slightly parted after speaking, and considered the alternatives. He was fine with listening to her tales of Ewan and the alternative of kissing her until she could no longer speak. Stopping with just a kiss didn't seem reasonable. He rested his chin on his forearms.

"Tell me about my son."

>>>>><<<<<

Iseabal fell into bed exhausted, yet at peace. Her doubts, long plagued by the consequences of loving her English knight and fueled by an uncertain future with a child who could claim no father, had disappeared during the long hours as she regaled Simon with tales of their son.

I'm glad ye will get to know him, Simon. Glad Ewan has such a good man to call father.

Ripples of unrest kept her from dropping into sleep. Throughout the evening, Simon had claimed her with light touches to the back of her hand, a knuckle softly brushing her cheek, igniting sparks of anticipation along her skin. The press of his thigh against hers through chemise, gown, and surcoat had kept her shivering with need. He'd played the smitten swain well.

And left her at the door to her chamber with a chaste kiss and bid *gentle night.*

She hugged her pillow against her chest, imagining the warmth of Simon's body next to hers.

"Sheep bollocks. 'Tisnae the same." She flung the pillow aside then flopped onto her back to stare at the canopied hangings above the bed. Footsteps tramped the short hallway outside her room, then were silent. The fire crackled on the hearth. Moonlight shifted through the narrow window as clouds gathered. Iseabal sighed deeply and resolutely closed her eyes. The light, sweet fragrance of the yellow iris in a pitcher near the bed teased her nose.

Flowers. He gave me flowers. Iseabal smiled, remembering the tiny sprig of gorse he'd presented her five years ago, his fingertips bruised and scratched from grasping the thorny leaves.

Had I known it carried thorns, I would have left it to its shrubbery. His voice rueful, he'd shaken his head and handed the pretty yellow flowers to her, then stuck his thumb in his mouth.

Iseabal moaned and flopped onto her belly, burying her face into her crossed arms.

Deep breaths. Slow, deep breaths.

Heated thoughts of Simon faded.

How peculiar it is to have a bed to myself. To not share with a wean who kicks and sprawls across the mattress. She relaxed. *Ahh.* A forgotten luxury.

One she'd trade for the weight of Simon next to her.

'Tis my decision. He's nudged me all evening to tell him aye, yet he wouldnae force my agreement.

She rolled slowly to her side and stared at the pulsing embers on the hearth, diverted by the plight of the serving lass, Rosaline.

Poor lass. Her betrothed killed these few days past by James and his men. And her the eldest of five lasses. Sent here weeks before her wedding to get her out of the way of the others.

Now, unwed and unwanted by her betrothed's bereaved parents, she had nowhere to turn. Choices were being forced upon her. To linger as an impoverished servant at North Hall, or to accept the offer of a middle-aged crofter with three young children.

My choices are much better.

Simon. I truly never thought to see ye again. And for a time, I rather hoped I would—though ye may not have liked the result.

She sighed again. *I have a chance for a home, a family, and a man I love—and who is doing his best to court me.*

Warmth rolled through her, sending her surging to her feet. She swept the confining blankets away and stomped them into submission beneath her bare feet.

Taking a moment to pull a thick robe about her shoulders, she walked to the door and pulled it open, then stepped into the hall.

SIMON PACED THE floor before the hearth. The peat fire blazed, pushing the cold night air to the corners of the chamber. It scarcely registered with Simon as a different fire burned inside, consuming him, demanding he march to Iseabal's room and remind her how the passion had flared between them. How she'd once melted in his arms and made him forget he'd been sent to capture Scottish reivers, not seduce Scottish lasses.

Not just any lass. *His* lass with hair the color of a starless night, skin the color of palest pink roses, and a forthright kindness that went straight to his heart.

He wanted her. Now. But damned if he was going to force her to accept him. The memory of the chaste kiss he'd given her at the door to her chamber mocked him.

He strode purposefully to the door and gripped the latch, every muscle straining to take him to Iseabal's room. He halted. Stared at his hand. Releasing the latch, he drew his hand away, shoving his fingers through his hair in exasperated frustration.

The latch wiggled. Simon stared at it as if it was a snake. It wiggled again then clicked. With a sigh of well-oiled hinges, the door opened.

Glittering green eyes met his. Iseabal blinked as if startled to find him at the door. A smile tugged hesitantly at the corner of her mouth, a brow raised as if questioning her acceptance in his room.

Simon's blood thickened, his heart thudding heavily in his chest. With a small nod and a sweep of his arm, he invited her through the doorway. The hem of Iseabal's robe trailed behind her, twitching provocatively with each gentle sway of her hips.

Simon licked his dry lips and dragged his attention from Iseabal's sweetly rounded bottom. She halted near the hearth and faced him. He waited, wondering what had brought her to his room. Hoping she planned to stay. He wasn't certain he would allow her through the door again before morning.

"I dinnae wish to sleep alone."

Simon's eyes widened. With exaggerated calmness, he untied the laces of his tunic at cuff and neck. He released his belt and let it fall to the floor. Iseabal's gaze followed his actions, and as he hesitated, she slid her fingers through the loose ties of her robe, then pushed it from her shoulders, the cloth mirroring the fall of his belt.

"I wish to spend the night in yer arms, Simon."

Breath whooshed from Simon's lungs. He quickly shed his boots and linen undergarments, leaving only his tunic which hung nearly to his knees. The cloth, soft as a woman's breath, slid across his erect cock. He stifled a groan.

Once committed, Iseabal's fingers flew, raking open the neckline of her thin night rail, sending it to the same fate as her robe. Simon stripped his tunic over his head and tossed it onto the growing pile of clothing.

Iseabal stood naked before him. "Remind me how good we were together."

Firelight silhouetted her body, turning her pale skin to a dusky shade of gold, hiding and flaunting her contours at the same time. Simon stepped before her and took her hands, turning her so the smoldering embers cast their glow onto her, proving his memory a poor match for the reality of the woman before him.

He cleared his throat. "Ye do not have to do this. No matter if ye accept my offer or not, ye and Ewan will always have my protection."

Iseabal drew a groaning, shuddering breath and touched a forefinger to his lips. "Hush, Simon, and kiss me."

CHAPTER SEVENTEEN

'TWAS BETTER THAN she remembered. She'd been naught but a lass five years earlier, frantic with the need to convince Simon to take her with him. Full of impossible expectations gleaned from innuendos and whispers she had not understood. She'd been so young, unprepared for the overwhelming wholeness of giving herself to Simon. The devastation she'd experienced when she'd woken to find him gone had effectively buried the memory of the pleasure they'd shared.

This time he was hers. He'd offered her more than a single night—he'd offered her himself, his love, and his name. Her belly tightened, wanting him again, wanting to wake him with caresses that explored every inch of him and brought him to the brink of passion. She wanted to push him over that edge, hear her name on his lips as he surrendered to the power that never ceased to surprise her.

How naïve to believe their kisses of yesterday signified the bond between them. This hunger to possess him and to have him possess her was completely unfathomable. Yet it ignited a hunger she could not deny.

"I want ye again," he whispered, turning on his side to press against her.

Iseabal gasped as Simon's cock burned against her thigh. His fingers sought the curve of her breast, the rough pad of his thumb flicking across her sensitive nipple.

"I do not wish to hurt ye, but I do not believe I can get out of this bed until I have ye once more."

Iseabal rolled to face him and scooted close, draping a leg over his hips. He hitched forward, touching her core gently, seeking entrance and groaned as he slipped slowly inside her. Iseabal shifted, helping him sink deep. Her eyes closed as she gave herself to the ancient rhythm that fired her blood and sent her breathless to her release.

SIMON SHIFTED IN his chair, half-annoyed with the discomfort of a seemingly perpetually hardened cock.

Just the thought of Iseabal sent heat flooding his groin, and sitting across the small table from her as she placed a piece of bread in her mouth was enough to challenge his intent to allow her to finish breaking her fast before whisking her off to bed again.

"I'd thought of taking ye riding today to see the land around North Hall," he said, averting his gaze for a moment to give himself a chance to batten down his randy response every time he looked at Iseabal. He grabbed a mug of ale and took a sip.

"That might not be the best idea," she murmured. "Not that I dinnae love riding and miss my pony at Eaglesmuir something fierce."

Simon glanced up as she shrugged. Her cheeks pinked and she shifted beneath his gaze.

"I dinnae believe I could sit long in a saddle this morn."

He wanted to feel remorseful, but the twinkle in her eye told him she'd enjoyed the night's activities as much as he had. A grin slipped across his face and Iseabal laughed.

"A shame yer cock isnae sore this morn," she complained. "From the way ye're leering at me, I can tell ye would have me on my back in a trice if ye thought I'd stand . . . er, lay still for it."

"From what I recall, ye did not lay still last night."

Iseabal's cheeks flamed. "'Twasnae possible." She shifted in her seat. "Ye like it when I move—like that?"

"Faith, woman!" Simon exclaimed, shocked she seemed to have no notion how her movements and sounds affected his pleasure. "Ye have no idea?"

Of course she does not know. Though she was not a virgin last night, she was all those years ago, and I'd bet my war horse she's not slept with a man since.

He rose and stepped to her side. Taking her hands, he drew her to her feet.

"Everything about ye pleases me, my heart. And especially when I have ye so twisted up ye cannot help yerself." He leaned closer. "I feel the same about ye, Iseabal. I cannot imagine not waking next to ye."

"Aye. I need to be next to ye, as well. I will marry ye, Simon."

"And give me a wee daughter with eyes the color of emeralds and hair like black silk?"

Iseabal's eyes danced. "Or mayhap with golden curls like her da?"

"Hmm. Mayhap. Are ye ready to try?"

"Faith, Simon! We've already tried a half-dozen

times!" She tilted her head, her fingers curling against his palms. Yet a tentative smile dimpled her cheeks.

With a snort of laughter, Simon hugged her close.

"Nae, we do not have to put all our efforts into enlarging our family this day. My heart is full of you and Ewan. We can certainly find other diversions."

Iseabal tucked her head against his shoulder. "In less than a day I have discovered my heart has been ever in yer keeping these past years. With ye I am safe; my home is where ye are."

"I swear I will never fail ye again, Iseabal. My life and my future are yours to command."

⤜⟫⟫⟫⟪⟪⟪⤛

"TIME TO WAKE up, Master Ewan."

The soft voice reminded Ewan of his ma, but he knew his ma wasn't here. Aggie should be close by, but he didn't hear her snores. He reached for Shep, burrowing his hand in the dog's thick, soft fur. Shep licked his face and whined. The bed curtains were still drawn, and Ewan could see little more than the faint glow of the dog's white ruff.

"I'll have Cook make an extra pasty for ye if ye come along like a good boy."

A corner of the bed curtains parted and Ewan recognized the face of a woman Auntie Marci didn't like much. She was pretty, with yellow hair almost the color of his da's. But Auntie Marci had not spoken with her much the day before, and had given her one of the adult stares he knew meant she was displeased. A bit of sympathy tugged at Ewan's heart. He'd been in trouble before and knew how sad it made him. Mayhap she only wanted a friend.

He sat up, still a bit wary, but liking the promise of an extra pasty. And before breaking his fast. His tummy rumbled.

The woman smiled. "There ye are, sweet child. And already awake." She stood, pulling aside the curtain, a finger to her lips.

"Be as silent as ye can. Your nurse is still sleeping. I'm to play with ye until she wakes."

Ewan rubbed his eyes then leaned forward, accepting the soft hand the woman offered. He wiggled down from the bed, and Shep leapt down beside him, pausing to stretch first his front then his back half. A toothy yawn and shake of his head and shoulders that rippled all the way to his bushy tail, and Shep was ready to go. Ewan smiled and gripped Shep's ruff.

"Let's leave the doggie with Aggie," the woman whispered. "That way he can help her find us once she wakes."

Ewan balked. "I dinnae wish to leave Shep." His fingers tightened in the fur and Shep whined. "He's my friend."

"I will be your friend this morn. Do not worry. He's going to help your nurse."

A frisson of unease slid through Ewan. He jerked his hand from the woman's grip. "Nae! I want Aggie!" His voice rose and he darted across the room to bury his face in Aggie's lap as she sat beside the fire. She was not there. Ewan halted, confused. Afraid. Aggie was always there.

A hand grabbed Ewan's shoulder and jerked him backward, burying him in layers of cloth. Dragged across the floor, Ewan found himself outside his room. The door slammed against Shep's angry barks, reducing the noise to only faint protests.

Ewan wiggled furiously, trying to find his way out of the woman's grip. He shouted, but the sound was lost in the woman's skirts. She yanked his arm, spinning him about, and shoved a wad of cloth into his open mouth. His eyes widened, meeting brown ones sparkling with malice. He kicked, meeting her legs with nothing more than his bare feet. Tears of pain sprang to his eyes. He froze, terrified, unable to understand what was happening.

With a deft turn, his captor spun him about once more, tying a strip of cloth about his face, holding the wad in place behind his teeth. He gagged. He reached up to grab it, to yank it away, but she wrapped another strip about his wrist, pulling a knot tight with a single tug.

"Do not make me hurt ye, little boy," she snarled, leaning close.

Ewan butted her face with the top of his head and she cried out, losing her grip on his arm. Snatching free, Ewan darted past. With an angry grunt, the woman grabbed the back of his sleep tunic and jerked him against her side, wrapping her arm about his neck to pin him in place. He kicked and moaned but she held him tight as she tied his hands together then dragged him before her.

"I will send someone to kill your dog if ye do not behave." Her voice fell to a wheedling whisper. "No one wishes to hurt ye, and ye could be back by supper if ye do as ye are told." She straightened, hand on his shoulder, fingers gripping like talons.

"Will ye come quietly?"

Heart racing, eyes brimming with tears, Ewan shook his head.

With deliberate aim, he pissed on the bad woman's skirts.

⋙⋘

THE FAINT PEARLED line around the narrow window told Iseabal dawn was near. She couldn't remember being so content, so utterly boneless with the desire to remain abed and allow the world around her to continue without challenge or design. If she were a cat in the stable, she was certain the entire keep would hear her purr.

"Shall we wait until tomorrow for your sister to return with Ewan?"

Simon's voice, deep with arousal from sleep and other activities they'd indulged in the long night, rolled over her, warm and honeyed. She glanced up, a curious mix of *aye* and *nae* crossing her tongue.

"I dinnae know what to say. I miss him terribly, yet find myself enjoying ye entirely too much."

"'Tis impossible to enjoy me too much," Simon

teased, drawing a finger from the tip of her nose to bump lightly over the rise of her lips—a heated line over her chin and throat, changing to a full palm sliding across her breasts.

She sucked in a deep breath of pleasure. Simon kissed her lightly and rose from the bed.

"We could spend a night at Belwyck and return here on the morrow, in time for the wedding and Cook's feast."

Iseabal sighed. "I suppose 'tis time to act as there is aught more to life than lying abed, being waited on hand and foot." She flung back the covers and swung her legs over the edge of the mattress. Interest flared instantly in Simon's eyes.

"'Tisnae fair to restrict an active man like ye to a single room," she murmured as she rose, leaving her robe to dangle from one hand, dragging the boards as she crossed the floor to kneel beside the wooden chest beneath the window. The fall of early morning sun's rays across her shoulders was no accident, and she could almost hear Simon's heartbeat double its pace from across the room.

She flung open the lid and grabbed the gown on top, deciding to take pity on her husband to be. For the nonce, at least.

"I'll have hot water sent up," Simon said, attempting to shove a leg into his breeches for the third time—and missing yet again. "If we leave within the hour, we should arrive at Belwyck before the noon meal."

"I will be ready," Iseabal assured him.

He at last yanked his breeches to his waist and fumbled with the laces. She smiled as he shrugged into his tunic and dropped a kiss to her forehead before slipping through the door. The latch caught with a snick.

Iseabal put together a bag of her belongings as she waited on her bath. She pinned up her hair, deciding to wait to wash it, knowing it would take too long to dry for them to be away in the hour, and knowing Marci would want to help her prepare for her wedding day. Tendrils damp from her ablutions clung to the back of her neck as she dressed, drying quickly in the heat from the hearth. She twisted a couple of locks about her forefinger, leaving them to curl on either side of her face.

Simon returned to the room moments later. "Ye are beautiful," he murmured against her neck. "I am lucky to have found ye again."

Iseabal faced him, stepping into his embrace. Her arms encircled his waist, hugging him close. "I am glad ye did."

His cock rose between them and Iseabal smothered a smile as she stepped back. "Are ye ready to leave?"

He sent her a wry grin and a wink as he gathered a clean tunic from the chest and dumped it into her bag. Closing the drawstring, he flipped the bag over his shoulder. He held out his hand and Iseabal slipped her palm against his.

"I am now."

CHAPTER EIGHTEEN

I SEABAL EYED THE gathering clouds overhead. "How much farther?"

Simon glanced up, squinting his eyes. "An hour, mayhap more." He tilted his head. "I'm very sorry, love, but I believe we're going to get wet."

Iseabal frowned, though she knew there was naught to be done. "The sky appeared promising this morn," she noted. A shiver ruffled through her in anticipation of the rain to come.

Her mount snorted and shied at a dry leaf blown across the path. Iseabal gripped the saddle tight between her legs and patted the horse's neck.

"Easy, Drue," she murmured. "Ye'll be in a dry stall anon. Dinnae fash at the wind."

"She appears a bit flighty today," Simon remarked. "Not at all like herself. Her name means *courage* in Greek."

"Ye could have given her the Greek word for *feard-*

ie and I'd not know the difference," Iseabal laughed. The mare settled beneath Iseabal's calming touch, her hoofbeats regaining their easy rhythm. She tossed her black mane, her dapple gray hide rippling across taut muscles, gleaming with health and power.

"She's a beauty," Iseabal said. "I love her long legs and the slope of her hocks which make her so easy to ride."

"I thought the same of ye this morn."

Iseabal's neck and cheeks flamed. She didn't need a bit of mirrored steel to know her face burned bright red. Uncertain whether she should be outraged or amused at Simon's unexpected words, she bit her lip. Mirth won and she laughed. Men astride great war horses on either side glanced at her, too far away to have heard Simon's banter. She hoped. Her face flamed hotter.

The sky darkened and she silently thanked the thickening clouds for covering her embarrassment. Yet a thrill of feminine power fluttered in her belly and she hid her small smile.

Dense woods rose ahead, branches swaying in the freshening wind.

"We may have a bit of shelter once we reach the

trees." Simon's voice whipped away on a gust. Iseabal ducked her head against the first drops of rain. They urged their horses faster and entered the forest just as a crash of thunder announced the downpour. The road quickly became a morass of churned mud that spattered Iseabal's skirts with every flick of her horse's hooves.

She pulled the hood of her cloak further forward, shielding her face from the worst of the rain, and hunched forward to help drain the water pooling in the lap of her ruched skirts. Morning mists wound through the trees, giving reluctant way to the rain and the press of warm bodies breathing steam into the crisp air. A roll of thunder rumbled up the trail.

"To Iseabal!"

Simon snatched Iseabal's horse's reins, hauling both animals to a halt before the words were out of his mouth. Iseabal grabbed the saddle, jolting to one side at the sudden stop. Fear doubled the beat of her heart. Knights surrounded her and Simon, muscled horses and drawn blades forming a stout wall about them. Her stomach dropped.

More shouts and the clank of steel rose. Horses whinnied. Simon wrested his mount from the safety of his knights and rode to the head of the column of approaching riders where two mounted men awaited. A dog leapt against the restraint of his lead.

Hunters?

The gray veil of rain blurred the images, but there was a familiarity that struck Iseabal. She urged her mare as close as the surrounding knights and horses would permit. Could it be Lord de Wylde and Walter? Her gaze settled on the dog, his coat plastered to his sides, black with a bit of white at the neck.

Shep?

SIMON'S HEART MISSED a beat. He'd not sent word of their travel. Why would The Saint and Walter meet them on the road? With Ewan's dog? A chill ran through him that had nothing to do with the cold rain.

Lord de Wylde wasted no words. "Your son is missing."

Simon exhaled on a whoosh of air, his stomach twisting as if he'd received a physical blow. "When?"

"Not two hours past."

"God's bones. What happened?" Simon glanced quickly over his shoulder, making certain Iseabal was far enough away to not overhear them.

"Someone heard a ruckus coming from the boy's room just before dawn. When they opened the door, the dog, which never leaves his side, leapt past. The barking woke everyone within hearing, including myself and Lady de Wylde. Our room is down the passageway from his." Geoffrey nodded to the dog. "He's led us here, apparently seeking Ewan."

"Anything else ye can tell me?"

Geoffrey hesitated, exchanging looks with Walter. Shep barked, fighting against his leash.

My son is missing.

Simon withered the recalcitrant pair with a glance. "Anything!"

"Kaily is also gone."

"Shite!"

"What is wrong?" Iseabal's voice crossed the distance between them.

Dread gutted Simon. He wheeled his horse and spurred him to her side, Lord de Wylde and Walter at his heels.

"Ewan is missing. Shep will lead us to him."

Pray God we're not too late.

Iseabal whitened and swayed in her saddle.

"We will find him, my heart."

Or die trying.

"I'm going with ye."

Simon frowned. "Ye cannot keep up."

Her eyes flashed. "Dinnae try to keep me from my son."

❈❈❈

"I WANT MY money *and* a new gown. Look at what the brat did!"

The bad woman's voice shook, growling deep and angry. Her grip tightened on Ewan's arm.

"Hand the lad over." A man with a scowl reached for Ewan. Ewan shrank back and the bad woman snatched him from the man's grip.

"Not until ye give me the money ye promised. Ye'll not have an easier way to get his ma than with him. But he's caused me more trouble than he's worth and I can take him back to Belwyck as easily as hand him over if ye think to cheat me." She bumped Ewan aside, yanking her skirt from beneath his feet.

He stumbled, tears welling. His feet hurt, he was frightened, and he didn't know where Shep was. Shep always helped him when he was scared, and the bad woman had shut him in the room and made him stay behind. Could he still be there?

He frowned to keep from crying. He was a big boy, and no matter what happened, he was *not* going to cry. His da would want him to be strong. He *was* strong, though he was also very tired. Ewan rubbed his face on his shoulder. His wrists hurt, too. He needed to pee again, but wasn't certain he wanted to make the bad woman angrier.

Their voices grew louder. Ewan squinted. The man looked familiar, but he didn't know his name. Only his angry voice made him remember the night his grandda died. He'd been an angry person, too.

Thunder rumbled and fat raindrops pelted Ewan's hair. Chill bumps rose on his skin as the rain soaked through his tunic. The others huddled beneath their cloaks. Ewan shivered. A bead of water ran down his forehead and dripped from the end of his nose. He wanted his ma. When would his da come get him? Tears blended with the rain.

"Give the *frowe* what we owe her," the man growled. He crossed his arms over his chest, fingers twitching.

A second man stepped close, a hand beneath his cloak. The hilt of a dagger protruded from the draped edge of the cloth. Ewan's eyes widened. Before he realized what was happening, the man struck the woman in the belly, jerking his hand upward so hard her feet left the ground. He drew his fist back, steel winking like rain in the gloom. The woman crumpled to the mud and did not move.

Ewan whimpered, his gaze sliding to the first man who grinned with evil satisfaction.

"Stupid cow won't need a new kirtle, now, will she?" He turned to Ewan and scowled. "Get this wee scunner bundled up and on a horse. 'Twould be unfortunate if he became feverish and died before I get his ma."

The second man stepped toward Ewan. Ewan backed away, determined not to let him close enough to use his dagger as he'd done to the bad woman. His retreat met with something solid behind his back. It shifted as he touched it with his bound hands and he realized it was the leg of a horse. Ducking, Ewan slipped under the horse's belly.

"Come, now, laddie," the man wheedled. "Dinnae cause a stramash."

Ewan stared at him, voiceless. The man grabbed the horse's reins and hauled the beast to the side. The horse snorted and took a step backward. Ewan butted the horse's side. The horse jerked his head against the pull of his reins, prancing at the abuse. One hoof landed on the man's foot.

"Shite!" He shoved the horse away and advanced on Ewan, the glitter in his eyes promising punishment.

Ewan slid around the rear end of the horse, his shoulder against the animal's quivering haunch. The man followed, slapping the horse's butt to move him. Ewan drove his shoulder into the horse's flank, misjudging his dive to escape beneath the horse's belly. Ears flattened, the horse lashed out with a hind leg, his hoof catching the man mid-thigh. A sharp clap rang out. The man screeched and collapsed to the ground.

"Ye wick!" The first man rushed to his friend's side and knelt in the mud. The injured man shrieked and arched his back, but he did not rise.

A dog barked.

Ewan whirled. He blinked his eyes against the rain and gloom and peered into the woods.

"Shep?"

A hand grabbed Ewan, twisting his arm, jarring his shoulder. He cried out at the pain.

"Yer ma will find a dead son when she comes for

ye," the man snarled as he dragged Ewan across the glen.

"No!" Ewan shouted. He twisted and struggled. Collapsing forced the man to drag him, but he did not stop. A dog's growl rumbled. A whistling sound cleaved the air. Ewan's captor released his grip and grasped his throat, a gurgling sound frothing from his lips.

"Ewan!"

He glanced up. Shep darted past to nose the man's still form then returned to Ewan, prancing and barking with excitement. Ewan grabbed Shep's fur and hugged the dog close.

"Ewan." His da dismounted his horse and seized Ewan, pulling him close. Ewan sagged against him, feeling warm and safe. After a moment, his da drew back. "Are ye hurt?"

Ewan shook his head. Drawing a knife, his da cut the bindings on his wrists then lifted him in his arms. Ewan nestled his face against his da's neck and hung on for dear life.

SIMON BURIED HIS face against his son's shoulder. A shudder ran through him.

My God. I thought I was too late. Grief, despair, anger, and anguish flooded him, weakening his arms and legs. What if he'd been an instant slower to arrive? Ewan's captor had drawn his sword, two others lay dead or wounded on the ground. He'd not had time to think. What if his dagger had missed the villain's throat? There had been no other target available.

Pain tore through his stomach, ripping upward, piercing his heart. He tightened his grip on Ewan.

I could have lost him forever.

Hands tugged at him. Simon turned his back to the person trying to take Ewan from him.

"Give me my son!"

CHAPTER NINETEEN

I SEABAL'S VOICE CUT through Simon's resistance and he pivoted to face her. Rain streaked her face like tears, her arms outstretched, demanding her child.

He is her child. She carried him, birthed him, and has raised him for more than four years without my help.

Ewan reached for his ma. Abruptly, Simon shoved the boy into Iseabal's arms.

"Get them on a horse and to Belwyck!"

Knights hurried to their side, bustling Iseabal to her horse. Within a few moments, they were gone, the sound of hooves on the muddied ground a muted rumble.

"My lord, this man and woman are dead." Sir Richard nodded to the third, some strides away. "He lives, though his upper leg is shattered."

Lord de Wylde stepped forward. "Throw him on a horse and get him to Belwyck. We will question him there." He glanced at Simon. "Join me."

He spun on his heel and mounted his horse. Surrounded by his personal guard, The Saint galloped from the clearing.

"My lord?" Sir Richard gave Simon a questioning look. "We await your orders."

Still in a fog of uncertainty, Simon glanced about, his gaze lingering a moment on the man at his feet.

James Maxwell? He would know soon.

He moved to the damp pile of skirts, blonde hair darkened by the rain and sliding into the obscurity of the puddle surrounding her body.

Kaily.

Deciding he'd seen enough, he returned to his horse. "Let's get out of here."

>>><<<

ISEABAL TIGHTENED THE laces on her gown, then pulled the surcoat over her head. The beautiful blue wool, so soft it felt like velvet, belonged to Marci, and Iseabal appreciated both the warmth of the garment and of her sister's spirit. Though she'd changed into clean, dry clothes, her center remained frozen with a cold no fire or cloak could thaw.

She couldn't get enough of Ewan's touches and glances, realizing he derived comfort from her presence. She could not let him out of her sight, rubbing him dry, dressing him in a sleep tunic, listening to his breathing as she wrapped him in a thick wool blanket. Marci had moved his belongings to a different chamber, understanding his likely reluctance to return to a room where his safety had been violated.

Aggie, wobbly from a blow to her head, had been discovered behind the privy screen in Ewan's room and sent to a darkened chamber by order of the healer who set a lass to watch over her.

Marci gathered Iseabal's hair and finger-combed it into sections. With practiced hands, she braided the locks. "I am so sorry, Izzy."

"There is naught to be sorry for. How could ye know Kaily would do such a thing?"

Marci shook her head, the movement caught dimly in the polished bit of metal hanging on the wall. "'Twill always be on my heart. Poor lad. Och, Izzy, I'm so sorry."

Iseabal glanced at Ewan who curled next to Shep on the dog's blanket by the hearth, his chest rising and falling in a slow, peaceful cadence. He'd finally fallen asleep after asking for his da half a dozen times.

"Will ye stay with him? I'd like to find Simon."

"Of course. I willnae leave his side." Marci patted Iseabal's hand. "Check the hall. Mayhap someone saw him come in."

Then why has he not come to see me or Ewan?

Iseabal frowned at Simon's absence, then gave Marci a hug. With a nod, she grabbed a shawl and left the room.

⸎

Ignoring the stable boy's offer, Simon dismounted and led his horse into the stable and found an empty stall. He'd rather be back at North Hall, but Lord de Wylde had demanded his presence at Belwyck. Simon would remain only long enough to hear what their prisoner revealed.

He added a scoop of oats to his horse's trough, then grabbed a rough cloth to dry his belly and sturdy legs, removing as much of the mud as possible. He'd brush the rest out after it dried.

With a groan, Simon backed to the stone wall. He slid down its length, landing on his buttocks in the hay. He leaned his forehead on his knees.

God! He'd nearly lost Ewan. Great shudders wracked him, unstoppable no matter how hard he tried.

I promised Iseabal no harm would come to him.

He drew a deep breath and stared sightless into the dimly lit stable, hearing the rustle of rain through the thatched roof, but the comfort of the gentle sound was denied him.

"Simon?"

He hesitated then rose to his feet.

"Simon." Iseabal's hand rested on the top of the half door. Drops of rain glistened in her hair, on her lashes, and on the shawl draped over her shoulders. He sent her a slight nod then returned to grooming his horse. "Come inside. I'll fetch ye a warm drink and dry clothes. Ye mustnae remain out here."

"I will be heading back to North Hall soon. Do not worry over me."

"Then I will see that Ewan and I are ready." She turned to leave.

"No."

Iseabal halted, pivoting slowly to face him.

"I beg yer pardon?"

"I release ye from your promise."

"What are ye saying?"

"I will see to it ye receive more than adequate support. Even should ye marry, ye and Ewan will want for naught."

Iseabal wrenched the door open and stormed through. "Oh, no ye dinnae, Simon de Bretteby! Ye walked away from me once, and I willnae allow it to happen again."

Simon's fist shot into the air. "Ye should be the one walking away, not me!" he shouted. "I nearly got him killed!"

Iseabal's eyes flashed. "Ye did nothing of the sort! Ye saved him."

"I promised ye he would come to no harm. I should have been able to protect him."

"Well, pardon ye for not being God but merely a human who cannae see into the future," she snarled. "Ye are unbelievably arrogant to think ye could plan for every possibility."

"I am a knight. I have been trained since I was a lad. I should be able to see *every* possibility. Plan for them." He lowered his arm. "Guard against them."

"Ye did yer best."

"It wasn't enough."

"Do ye think I dinnae feel the same? I'm his ma!

The one who is supposed to care and watch for his safety. If ye failed him, then so did I."

Simon's mouth twisted as if he would argue with her.

"Ye saved Ewan." Iseabal's lips settled into a stubborn line.

"Ye were not there."

"Nae. Yer bloody big horse outran mine."

"He pulled a sword. On Ewan. I had to kill him."

"No one is lamenting James Maxwell's death," she retorted.

Simon stared past her, seeing the events again. Ewan. The glint of steel in the man's hand. "He was going to kill Ewan."

"Och, Simon!" Iseabal rushed against his chest, wrapping her arms about him. He stared at the top of her head. "Dinnae do this! Dinnae let James take ye away from me."

"He deserves better than me for a father." The words choked him, but they spoke the horrible truth in his heart.

Iseabal drew back slightly, and, against his will, his arms encircled her waist, pulling her back against him.

"Ye are his father. Ye will always have his good in yer heart. Today ye proved no one is better capable of protecting him. Ye were the only one there in time to save him. No one else could have done more."

His breathing eased as Iseabal's words soothed him. The fog consuming him lifted and he hugged her tighter.

"Dinnae tear us apart, Simon," she whispered. "I dinnae wish to be with anyone but ye."

He swallowed and eased his grip, tilting his head to study Iseabal's face. "I have never felt this way before. As if my heart could be ripped from my body—and I have no control over it."

"'Tis called love, Simon. Not infatuation, or the memory of a lass ye swived five years ago. But the love that binds ye to another's soul."

She drew her fingers across his cheek. "I wish ye could protect us from everything, Simon, but there will be times when our best may not conquer whatever ills have befallen us. Promise me ye willnae turn from me. Promise ye will always allow us to comfort each other."

He nodded. "I have known him less than three days, and already he is part of me."

Iseabal's smile lit his heart. "Do ye know what he said before he fell asleep?"

Simon shook his head.

"He wanted to see his da."

EPILOGUE

Four months later

ISEABAL BEAMED AS Simon planted a kiss on her cheek. He yelped loudly as Ewan dashed across the floor and plowed into his legs. Ewan giggled with delight and Simon scooped him up, lifting him high and giving him a playful shake before setting him back on his feet.

"Again!" Ewan chanted, lifting his arms.

Simon tickled the boy's oxter until Ewan shrieked with laughter.

"Can I go riding with ye, Da?"

With a lifted brow, Simon deftly tossed the question to Iseabal. "What do ye think, Izzy?"

She waved a hand in the air. "Off with ye and take the lad with ye. 'Tis a fine midsummer day and he needs to be outside." Glancing at her lightly rounded belly, she wiggled her feet. "I'm going to relax a bit today I think."

"Are ye well?" Concern knitted Simon's eyebrows together.

"Och, nary a thing to worry over. I've months to go before the bairn makes an appearance. Just feeling a bit lazy this day. Run on. Rosaline will care for me should I need anything."

Iseabal watched indulgently as Simon helped Ewan into his boots. With a wave and a shout of good-bye, they were gone, leaving behind blissful silence.

She sighed and turned to Rosaline.

"They'll be gone 'til noon if I have my guess. Plenty of time for ye to tell me what's bothering ye."

"M'lady?" Rosaline's crystal blue eyes widened.

"Och, dinnae dissemble, lass. Ye are punctual with yer tasks, and never a cross word, yet I havenae seen ye smile, nor do ye spend time with the others. I couldnae ask for a kinder maid, yet yer heart isnae in it."

Rosaline glanced down, folding her hands in her lap. Iseabal knew the motions—look away to keep from showing emotion and rest your hands in your lap to still their shaking. Something was amiss.

"Please let me help," Iseabal murmured. "It truly matters to me that ye are unhappy."

Rosaline's lips twisted, showing her indecision. Her unearthly eyes snapped to Iseabal's.

"The lad I was betrothed to is dead."

"Aye. Ye spoke of this to me three months past. Do ye not wish to remain here? I will help ye return to yer family if ye wish."

"I fear my da willnae welcome me back. I have four other sisters, as well as two younger brothers, and I was one mouth too many at the table. 'Tis why I was sent to live with James' family once the betrothal contract was signed. But James died a week before we were to wed, and his parents find me an unwelcome reminder of their loss. I chose to live at North Hall rather than under their accusing eyes."

"Why would they accuse ye? He was killed in a raid on the village. Ye had naught to do with that."

"Nae. The raid had naught to do with me. Though I truly dinnae look forward to wedding James." She glanced away again and her cheeks pinked.

"Then whyever did ye agree to the betrothal?"

Rosaline shrugged. "I dinnae expect the wedding to happen." She glanced from the floor to the hearth, and finally to Iseabal. "All the others have died."

Iseabal's eyebrows flew upward. "Saint Andrew's

stumpy toes, lass! How many men have ye been betrothed to?"

Rosaline's gaze slid away. "Including James? Three."

⫸⫷

SIMON DISMOUNTED AND handed his reins to a stable boy who led his horse away. Autumn leaves drifted lazily to the ground, bright gold offerings from a tree in a nearby garden. He dusted his hands on his breeches and strode to the main door of the keep while his personal guard scattered to the various vices of food, drink, or perhaps a game of dice in the soldiers' quarters.

Lord de Wylde met him at the top of the wide stone steps.

"How is your wife and babe?"

"Ewan grows apace, and so does the babe in Iseabal's belly—much like the one your wife carries," Simon noted blandly. A squeal of delight warned him an instant before Lady de Wylde grabbed his neck for a hug, her belly hindering the process. He bent good-naturedly to her kiss, knowing she'd not release him until he'd given her every assurance her sister was well and happy.

"Ye'll not beat her by many weeks," he teased, letting his gaze linger a moment on the mound her surcoat could not hide.

She smiled sunnily at him. "She is well? Ye dinnae let Ewan tire her?"

"My lovely wife is very content," he assured her. "Our only contention is whether the babe will be a boy or a girl. I'm hoping for a girl."

He offered her his arm and led her into the hall. Walter appeared before they'd taken many steps.

"Good to see ye, Simon. I wasn't certain your lady wife would let ye stray far from her side."

"Spoken like a man who has yet to find a woman to put up with him," Simon joked.

Marsaili rolled her eyes and released Simon's arm. "Men. I'm leaving now before ye rub knuckles on each other's heads."

Simon and Lord de Wylde laughed. Walter wore a troubled look. Lord de Wylde and Simon exchanged glances. Clearing his throat, Geoffrey de Wylde motioned to the other end of the enormous room.

"Come with me to my solar. We can discuss matters there in private."

Simon relaxed into a comfortable chair beside a long, narrow window where sunlight spilled across the floor. He stretched his legs out before him, pleased to be still and quiet for a moment.

"Something is on your mind, Walter. I can smell it from here."

Walter sent him a puzzled look then shook his head. Geoffrey took his seat at the large desk in the corner of the room and, deftly changing the topic, ignored Simon's quip.

"I'm sending a group of soldiers to Eaglesmuir to place a Johnstone in the keep. As per our discussions over the past couple of months, I've decided they will be our best allies in the area. My knights have already secured the keep, and they will turn it over to the new lord at the proper time."

"Laird Johnstone has agreed?"

"Aye. He'll support it until his son is old enough to manage on his own. Several families of Johnstones left Friar's Hill when my brothers took the village two years ago. This will give them a place to go if they wish, and shows I do not deal as my brothers did."

"'Tis a fair trade. Eaglesmuir is a fine keep near the River Annan."

"I'm still organizing men to help with the transition, and will be asking for one of my knights to volunteer to lead them in the next couple of days."

Simon shifted in his chair, his attention drawn to Walter's lack of interest. "What vexes ye, Walter? Ye've not said two words since we entered the room."

Walter frowned. "'Tis something ye mentioned a few months ago. I've been thinking on it lately . . . ."

"Ye are one of the most serious men I know," Simon remarked. "It has taken ye months to reflect on something I said . . . ."

Lord de Wylde raised a hand and Simon subsided his teasing.

"What is it, Walter?"

Walter shuffled his feet. "I don't know how I would handle a wife."

Simon hooted. "I know ye aren't a virgin, Walter."

Lord de Wylde sent him another quelling gesture.

Walter's face reddened. "That isn't what I meant. Housing. Food." He widened his hands, palms up. "Living."

"Ye have but to ask, Walter," Lord de Wylde replied. "There are a number of cottages within the walls of Belwyck that would do for a wife and family. Do ye have a lady in mind?"

Walter shook his head. "I have little to recommend me as a husband. I am a warrior, unversed in gentler arts."

Lord de Wylde lifted a brow. "Ye see before ye two warriors well-pleased with coming home to the *gentler arts* as ye put it."

Simon leaned forward. "There was a young woman at North Hall . . . ."

Walter glanced up, eyes widened. "Nae. She's beyond me."

"Walter, ye must banish that ridiculous notion. Any lady of North Hall would be pleased to marry a knight such as you."

Walter frowned. "Nae. She is betrothed. Likely wed by now."

Simon snapped his fingers. "Rosaline! Oh, sweet Rosaline! I fair remember her." He hesitated, his grin slipping away.

"What is wrong?"

"Her betrothed died in the raid at Friar's Hill when Iseabal first arrived."

Walter perked up noticeably. "Has she wed another?"

"No, at least, not to my knowledge. But she no longer resides in Friar's Hill."

"Where is she?"

"She has returned home—north across the Border. I believe her father is Laird Johnstone."

Book #3 in the Redeemed Trilogy coming soon!

ACKNOWLEDGEMENTS

I'd like to once again thank Kathryn Le Veque for inviting me on this journey in the World of de Wolfe. Life along the Scottish Border is fascinating!

I'm honored to also have my critique group along for this story. Cate Parke, Dawn Marie Hamilton, and Lane McFarland—I couldn't have done it without you!

And a huge thank you to Dar Albert for creating such a special cover for Iseabal and Simon's story.

From the Author

Thanks so much for your continued interest in the World of de Wolfe! Please consider leaving a review for the books you enjoy. It helps authors more than you know!

I love hearing from readers! You can find me on my website at www.cathymacraeauthor.com and there is a sign-up for my newsletter there, as well.

You can also find me on Facebook: cathy.macrae.58
Twitter: @CMacRaeAuthor
Pinterest: authorcathymacrae
and Instagram: @cathymacrae_author

Consider following me on my Amazon author page or Book bub where you'll receive notices on my new and discounted books.

More Books by Cathy MacRae

The Highlander's Bride Series:

The Highlander's Accidental Bride (Book 1)
The Highlander's Reluctant Bride (Book 2)
The Highlander's Tempestuous Bride (Book 3)
The Highlander's Outlaw Bride (Book 4)
The Highlander's French Bride (Book 5)

With DD MacRae
The Hardy Heroines series

Highland Escape (book 1)
The Highlander's Viking Bride (book 2)
The Highlander's Crusader Bride (book 3)
The Highlander's Norse Bride, a Novella (book 4)
The Highlander's Welsh Bride (book 5)
Mhàiri's Yuletide Wish (a Christmas novella)

The Ghosts of Culloden Moor series
with other authors

Adam (book 11)
Malcolm (book 16)
MacLeod (book 21)
Patrick (book 26)

Manufactured by Amazon.ca
Bolton, ON

24392376R00143